Dragos Cuelebre, Lord of the Wyr, needs to throw a party without maiming anyone.

That isn't exactly as easy as it might sound. After the destructive events of the last eighteen months, the Elder Races are heading to Washington D.C. to foster peace with humankind. Not known for his diplomacy skills, Dragos must rely on his mate Pia to help navigate a battlefield of words and polite smiles rather than claws. With Dragos's mating instinct riding close to the surface, his temper is more volatile than ever and the threat of violence hovers in the air.

Then the human spouse of a prominent politician winds up murdered and Dragos and Pia must race against time to hunt down those behind it before they are held responsible for the crime.

For fans of DRAGON BOUND and LORD'S FALL, the latest novella in the Elder Races holds passion, peril, political intrigue, and revelations that will change Dragos and Pia's lives forever.

DRAGOS GOES TO WASHINGTON is the first part of a three-story series about Dragos, Pia, and their son Liam. Each story stands alone, but fans might want to read all three in order as they will be released: DRAGOS GOES TO WASHINGTON, PIA DOES HOLLYWOOD, and LIAM TAKES MANHATTAN.

Dragos Goes to Washington

(A Story of the Elder Races)

Thea Harrison

Dragos Goes to Washington

ISBN 10: 0990666166
ISBN 13: 978-0-9906661-6-5
Print Edition

Chapter One

DRAGOS'S DENIM-CLAD, HARD thigh slid against Pia's as he sprawled back in his seat.

She wasn't wearing jeans. She wore shorts, and the small abrasive friction on her skin sent a frisson of sexual awareness thrumming through her body.

It was always that way between them. Heat shimmered whenever they were near each other, invisible yet intense. He burned up her world, until there was nothing else, nobody else but him.

The dragon would have been pleased to know it. Probably too pleased. He was demanding and possessive at the best of times, so she had no intention of telling him. He was in danger of becoming too complacent as it was.

The thought made her smile to herself. They must look very prosaic as they sat in the bleachers, just like the other parents, watching Liam practice on the football field with his teammates.

The kids were so adorable. Still in elementary school, their helmets were too big, their slim bodies undeveloped. Most were boys, but there were four intense girls on the field as well.

Other people were present and watching, several parents along with some of the other schoolchildren. Pia's heart constricted as her gaze lingered on one mother with two preschool children.

The mother handed a portable container of yogurt to the oldest, a delicate girl around three years old, who twirled to make the gauzy skirt of her sundress flare as she sucked on the mouthpiece of the container. She wore sparkly pink heart-shaped glasses. The smallest was a cheerful, fat baby in a stroller, wearing a floppy sunhat. Around six or seven months old, the baby gnawed busily on a teething biscuit.

The other parents were present to support the earnest players on the field, as they waited for football practice to end so they could take their children home.

She and Dragos were watching the practice to make sure they hadn't made a mistake in letting Liam join the team.

Since the school year had started, he'd had another growth spurt. It wasn't unusual for predator Wyr to grow at a faster rate than herbivores, but Liam's growth rate went far beyond that of a normal predator Wyr child. To minimize the strangeness of the situation for both Liam and his classmates, they had changed schools when they moved him up from first grade to fifth. The new elementary school was farther from home, but Pia didn't mind the extra driving time.

Sometimes she sent Eva ahead with the SUV, let Liam shapeshift into his dragon form, and rode on his shoulders as he flew the route to school. It was exactly as they had once said to each other—as soon as Liam had grown too big to ride her Wyr form, she could ride his.

The morning flights were their little secret. She was certain Dragos wouldn't approve, but Liam was so nervous at having a passenger who couldn't fly on her own that he flew slowly and with extreme care. Also, between the two of them, they had serious cloaking skills, so she always felt quite safe.

Once they reached a prearranged spot where they met Eva, behind a sheltered copse of trees out of sight from the road, Liam landed and shifted back into a boy. Pia would take the wheel and drive sedately the rest of the route, just like a normal mom taking her normal child to a normal school. They often giggled about that together.

Liam appeared to have adjusted well to the change in schools, and was so excited about the thought of joining the football team, that Pia hadn't had the heart to say no, even though she knew, watching him, that he was much faster and more powerful than any other child on the field.

That didn't dim his transparent joy at playing the game. She noted with approval how carefully he paced himself to match the other children's abilities.

"I think he's going to be fine, don't you?" She turned to Dragos.

"He's fine, as long as he doesn't lose his temper. He could hurt one of those other kids all too easily."

Dragos's voice was logical and matter-of-fact. He sounded like he was discussing the relative strengths and weakness of one of his sentinels.

She frowned at him. He had stretched out his long frame so that he sprawled over three aisles, leaning his elbows on the row of bleachers behind them with his boots propped on the row below.

The afternoon was bright and hot for early autumn, but Dragos never wore sunglasses as protection from the sun. He only wore them when he wanted to put a barrier between him and other people. They sat some distance from everybody else, so he had folded his sunglasses and tucked them into the pocket of his shirt.

Dressed in a plain gray polo shirt and jeans, his silken black hair and dark bronze skin appeared more burnished than ever. His gold eyes gleamed thoughtfully under straight, lowered brows. The only part of him that did not tan was the pale, thin scar that slashed across one brow.

The dragon was a creature of fire, and Dragos never burned, no matter how long he stayed out in the sun, while Pia had to constantly wear sunscreen on her pale skin, along with a baseball cap and sunglasses.

Suppressing an envious sigh, she said, "I hear what you're saying, but I don't think it's fair to judge him on what-ifs. He's a good, careful boy. If he says he can handle it, I think we have to believe him. We can't give him the experience of a happy childhood, brief though it may be, if we're always limiting what he can have or do. He would only grow to resent us, and rightfully so."

Dragos remained silent for a long moment. As usual, it was impossible to tell what he was thinking by the impassive expression on his hard features. After a time, he said, "He's advancing faster than we thought he would."

Unsure of where he was going with that statement, she replied cautiously, "I know."

Her husband sucked a tooth, the set of his mouth slanting as if he tasted something sour. His gold gaze cut sideways to her. "He's not going to be a boy too much longer. Maybe we should let him have that dog he wanted."

"Let him . . ." Her voice trailed away as she stared at him. "But you've always been so adamant against getting a dog."

He lifted one massive shoulder, powerful muscles rippling underneath the smooth gray surface of his shirt. "Yeah, well, I've thought about it some more and changed my mind. It would have to be a puppy, from a breed that's known for being calm, so we can train it not to panic whenever it's around me, Liam, or any of the sentinels."

Dragos truly did not understand the desire to have a pet. It was, he said, like how he couldn't understand Liam's love for the toy bunny he'd had since he was a baby.

Now, Liam had declared he was much too old for the bunny, although he still insisted on keeping it in his closet. If Liam wasn't so adamant on keeping it close, Pia would have stolen it from him by now.

She loved that bunny, tattered ears and all. She loved remembering how Liam had chewed on those ears as he was teething.

"What about when Liam's old enough to leave home?" she asked, giving back to Dragos his strongest argument. "That's going to happen faster than we could have thought. What are we going do with the dog then?"

He shrugged again. "I don't know. We can cross that bridge when we come to it."

Dragos tried so hard. Parenting was new to them both, especially parenting such a magically gifted child. But somehow it was different for Dragos. Pia was younger. In a lot of ways, she was more adaptable.

Dragos was . . . Well, to be honest, she wasn't sure how old he was. She just knew he was very old.

But he worked hard at overcoming that obstacle. As frightening and ruthless as he could be, he was an amazing father.

Her gaze drifted back to the happy, fat little baby in the stroller, and her heart constricted again. A strange, unknown force built in her chest, until she couldn't contain it any longer.

"I want another one." The words burst out of her before she had time to consider them, spilling out of a deep well of need she had barely acknowledged in herself.

"You want another what?" Dragos asked.

This wasn't the time to talk about such an emotionally charged subject. She tried to bite the words back, but they tumbled out anyway. "A baby. I want another baby."

"You want . . ." He stopped and started again, speaking his words with care. "You want to talk about that here?"

The astonished look on his face was too much to take. The details of the sunny late afternoon blurred as tears filled her eyes. Quickly, before Dragos could see her expression, she whipped around to face forward.

"No, of course not." Her voice shook. "I shouldn't have said that. It just fell out of my mouth."

He straightened from his slouching position.

If he touched her or showed any sign of gentleness, she could feel the tears would turn into a geyser, and she really didn't want to burst into tears in public. She really didn't.

What the hell, self?

Bolting upright, she slid away from him as she stuttered, "F-football practice is almost over—why don't you wait here for Liam, and I'll meet you both at the car?"

"Pia," Dragos said, the gold of his eyes flaring to incandescence. Clearly he didn't like that suggestion in the slightest.

Telepathically, she said, *Dragos, it's all right. I'm having an emotional moment. I didn't expect it. It came out of nowhere, and I'm a little embarrassed by it. I'd like to take a few moments to compose myself. Please.*

After a moment, he growled, *We're still going to talk about this.*

Of course we will. Just not in public, okay? Backing farther away, she headed down the wide concrete steps.

As she walked away, she could feel his fierce energy

boiling at her back. He hated it when she cried, and he would doubly hate the fact that she asked him to stay behind.

But he would do it, because she asked it of him. Because he loved her.

Aside from the small fact that he could be the most terrifying creature she'd ever laid eyes on, he was an excellent husband and mate as well as a father.

She reached the ground level. Just before she turned the corner, she looked back up at him.

No longer in a relaxed sprawl across the bleachers, he sat forward, bracing his elbows on his knees, his dark head angled toward her. He had put on his sunglasses, no doubt to hide the incandescence spilling from his gaze, and his jawline was tight. It made his hard, ruthless features look even fiercer.

Suddenly she noticed the incongruities in the scene.

It was a perfect suburban setting, on a perfect suburban day. Tame, emerald green fields rolled toward the town in the distance. The aged Adirondacks Mountains provided a picturesque backdrop.

The coach's whistle sounded over shouts and calls from the children. They ran toward him and stood in the group looking up as he talked to them.

Pia had been wrong about nobody paying attention to them.

Nobody had been paying attention to her.

Everybody paid attention to Dragos. As she glanced around, she saw several other adults peek up at where he sat, some distance away from anyone else.

He was the anomaly in the perfect suburban setting. He was a lion sprawling in the midst of a flock of plump, clucking pigeons, a dark, brutally elegant Mephistopheles taking a silent stroll through a placid country church, and some instinctive part of them knew it. A couple of the women looked frankly covetous. One in particular looked covetous and a little afraid at the same time.

As that described to a *T* the beginning of her relationship with Dragos, she understood exactly how that woman felt.

Pia didn't like to think of the lonely days when she had been forced to steal from Dragos, leave her life behind and go on the run. Those early days before she and Dragos had developed feelings for each other were some of her most uncomfortable memories.

She had been so frightened of him. Then, when she had met him, she had been so frightened *and* attracted to him at the same time, she had been one confused cookie.

He had been just as confused—angry at the theft, mistrustful, and sexually drawn to her at the same time. When he had first found her and tackled her on the beach, he had fingered her hair while examining her with that laser-sharp focus of his, and his erection had pressed against her hip.

So, is that your long scaly reptilian tail, or are you just happy to see me?

It had been the first thing she had ever said to him.

How on earth did we find ourselves here, of all places? she wondered as she looked around.

All at once the humor in the perfect suburban scene

struck her. As she walked toward their Cadillac Escalade, she found herself laughing and wiping her face at the same time.

ON THE TRIP home, Dragos remained silent.

Liam was full of excited chatter about his day, and the football practice, so he didn't notice anything odd.

However, Pia was excruciatingly aware of how quiet Dragos was. Nerves closed up her throat, and she responded to Liam just enough to keep the boy's momentum going, while she sneaked glances over at Dragos's hard, unrevealing profile.

He still wore his sunglasses. He wasn't hiding the expression in his eyes from her, was he? Biting her lip, she stared out her window at the passing scenery.

When they reached the house, they walked inside through the kitchen. Dragos told Liam, "Get yourself a snack. Your mom and I have something we need to discuss, so we're going up to our suite. We'll see you at supper."

"Sure." Liam glanced from Dragos to her. "Can I go swimming in the lake?"

Even though they had an Olympic-sized, heated swimming pool, Liam preferred swimming in the lake because he liked to dive for fish. Clearing her throat, she said, "Go right ahead. Let Hugh know, so he can go with you."

"Okay!" He opened the door to the fridge and stuck his head inside.

Turning to leave, Pia walked through the ground

floor and climbed the stairs on shaky legs. She knew exactly when Dragos left the kitchen to follow her, and not because she heard him. Even for such a big man, he could move in complete silence when he chose.

She could feel the heat of his Power when he came around the bottom of the stairs and drew closer. She picked up her pace until she was almost running down the hall. Leaving the suite door open, she looked around their untidy bedroom.

Clothes were strewn on the king-sized bed, suits for Dragos to wear, and her own outfits that she had laid along the edges of the bed and dropped various pieces of matching jewelry on top. None of her outfits were from Target, not for this trip.

She had forgotten that she was in the middle of packing. Sighing, she walked into her closet and dragged her largest suitcase off the shelf. As she walked back into the bedroom, Dragos stood in the middle of the floor, his hands on his hips, watching her. He had finally taken his sunglasses off.

Not quite looking at his face, she asked, "How long are we going to be in D.C. again?"

"I'm waiting on confirmation now, but it might be eight days, depending on when the demesne leaders meet," he said. "You should count on at least a week."

Packing for a week's stay in D.C. wasn't like packing for a week on vacation. She did some quick mental calculations.

She wouldn't be attending any demesne meetings between the leaders, so she dismissed that as irrelevant.

Seven days, with possibly three functions a day, meant she needed to think about taking as many as twenty-one outfits, and seven of those outfits needed to be evening wear. She might be able to get away with wearing the same outfit throughout the day, but she couldn't count on it.

One of those evening functions was a gathering she and Dragos were officially hosting at the Wyr residence in D.C., but other than designing and approving the menu with the Wyr event staff last week, thus far she hadn't had anything else to do except get ready for the trip.

Rubbing her eyes, she walked back into her closet, grabbed another suitcase and hauled it into the living room.

Other than his inky black eyebrows lowering in a frown, Dragos hadn't moved. He said, "Stop that."

"I can't, not if we're going to leave at eight in the morning." She dropped the second suitcase beside the first.

"It doesn't matter if we get a later start. Our first obligation isn't until tomorrow evening."

"The White House thing," she said. Sometimes her life boggled her mind. Once, never in a million years had she expected to attend anything at the White House as an invited guest.

"Yes, the White House thing. Come here." Quick as a cat, he snagged her arm and pulled her toward him.

She went over to him willingly enough, but somehow, as she got closer, her head grew heavier, until she was looking down at his feet.

Long, dark fingers curled underneath her chin and lifted her face gently.

At the same time, she lifted her gaze to meet his.

So many things had happened to them. Their relationship wasn't even two years old. Her pregnancy with Liam had happened as a result of their mating. Dragos didn't choose to become a father. He had adapted to it.

She told him, "Forget about my outburst of emotion at the school. I want you to know, whatever you say, it will be okay."

"Yes."

His response was so breathtakingly simple, at first it didn't register. When it did, her heart started to pound. She couldn't believe her ears.

"That's it—just yes?" she demanded, half laughing. "That's all you've got to say about it? I think I feel cheated out of a long, angsty conversation."

He raised one sleek eyebrow. "I didn't say that was all I had to say about it. I just thought I would cut to the chase." He studied her while he rubbed his thumb along the edge of her jaw. "You know as well as I do that the odds are against us. You also know that even if we do get pregnant, we would likely face many of the same challenges as we did the first time, and another baby isn't going to take Liam's place."

She shook her head. "Of course not. Liam is perfect just the way he is. Yes, it shook me at first to discover how fast he would mature, but I've dealt with that. Truly, that's okay."

"I believe you." He slid his hand away from her chin, his fingers caressing her neck. "And I believe that you want another baby for that baby's sake. Parenthood took us by surprise, and that's okay too. This time, though, I would like to make the choice."

"Exactly," she whispered. His touch began to drug her senses, soothing and arousing her at once, and she began to feel heavy for other reasons. Standing upright took more effort. Swaying forward, she spread her hands across the broad expanse of his chest.

He put his arms around her. "I think what we should talk about is how we will deal with the disappointment if it doesn't happen. Because chances are, it won't."

"You never know," she told him. She peeked up at his face. "There's no real rhyme or reason to how difficult it is for the Elder Races to conceive and carry children to term. Some families end up having more than one child. Maybe your sperm is so mighty, you shoot magic bullets."

His intent expression splintered, and he burst out laughing. Almost as quickly, he sobered again and told her with a completely straight face, "Of course I do."

Then it was her turn to laugh. She threw her arms around him. "Yes, we might be disappointed, and we'll deal with that if it happens. At least you want to try."

"I do." His voice deepened. As he cupped the back of her neck in one hand, he cupped the curve of her ass with the other. "Trying to get pregnant is one of my very favorite things to do. We'll have to practice frequently, and with great enthusiasm."

She snickered, while happiness danced inside. Maybe they would have a small intense girl with Dragos's gold eyes. Maybe they might have another dragon. She adored her fierce, loveable dragons.

There was still so much she wanted to talk about, and so much they needed to consider. As Dragos had pointed out, another child might very well have the same capabilities as Liam and grow at the same accelerated pace.

And as they had just both said to each other, there was also a very real chance they might not be able to get pregnant again. Liam had come as a result of their original mating frenzy. They might not be so lucky this time.

If that were the case, she wanted to consider adopting a Wyr baby. She would actually be happy to adopt any kind of baby, but their household and lives were so predominantly Wyr, she didn't want any child of hers to feel like an outsider, as she had when growing up.

But that could be saved for a future conversation. For now, her thoughts fragmented as Dragos ran a light finger underneath the neckline of her tank top. The tiny friction of his callused skin against hers caused a shiver to run down her body.

They might have a lot to talk about, but she had a feeling that, for now, the time for serious talking was over.

"We have a while until supper," he murmured. His gaze had turned heavy-lidded and predatory. "Perhaps we should start practicing to get pregnant."

She licked her lips. For the Wyr, contraception was not something they needed to do externally, like taking birth control pills or using condoms. Instead, it was an internal, inborn trait. Once, she had needed to use an IUD before she had managed to change into her Wyr form and fully access her Wyr side. Now, trying to get pregnant was as simple and fundamental as telling their bodies to let go.

Just let go.

It was a heady experience, like releasing the throttle on a high-speed engine. The need she felt for him never eased. It was a driving, unrelenting force that drove the definition of her days and nights. She had never been so obsessed about anything or anyone before. It had marked her so indelibly, she couldn't imagine living without it, without him.

Attempting to sound nonchalant, she said, "Yeah, I think you could use some pointers on that."

His eyes narrowed, and he tightened a massive fist around the delicate shoulder strap of her tank top, a gesture at once both very gentle and unabashedly dominant. "I'll make you eat those words."

"You are very welcome to try," she whispered. Her attempt at cockiness had turned breathy and yearning. "Please, try very hard."

A smile lit his hard features. "Trust me, that will be entirely my pleasure."

Chapter Two

THERE WAS NOTHING new to their banter. It was a staple of their daily lives, and Dragos had come to rely on it like he relied on breathing.

He basked in the sparkle that lit her eyes as if it were sunlight. Her happiness warmed and sustained him. Her feminine scent fed a ferocity of hunger that never faded or mellowed, no matter how he tried to sate himself on her.

Even when he had forgotten her completely, he had still wanted her. The memory of his brief spell of amnesia tightened his mouth.

The construction accident that had caused his injury had happened a few months ago. It had only taken him a few days to recover almost all of his memory, but even when he could have flown away from everything in his life and never known the difference, he had been fascinated by her presence and ensnared by her perseverance.

Even then, when the dragon had been at his most feral and dangerous, he had mated with her. He still remembered the strange, possessive struggle he had felt—the odd jealousy toward himself, or at least the man he thought he had been, before his memories had come flooding back.

They were twice mated. Old as he was, he had never heard of such a thing before. Using his grip on her spaghetti strap, he pulled her closer and growled softly into her face, "You'll never be rid of me. Never, as long as either of us live."

The same miracle occurred, as it always did, yet it never failed to astonish him. An expression of peace softened her features. She gave him a soft smile as she whispered back, "Never."

She wanted him to hold on. She wanted him.

He took hold of her hips and pressed her against him, so she could feel his erection straining against his jeans. Her eyelids grew heavy, and her peaceful expression grew flushed. She licked her lips, moistening the plump, soft flesh so that he had to taste her.

Bending his head, he covered her mouth with his. She had taught him how to be gentle, a trait that did not come naturally to him, but he had savored learning it, because it brought out all the many, delicate facets to her pleasure that he loved to devour.

The catch of her breath. The way her violet eyes darkened. The trembling of her lips. She was cooler than he, but even so, when passion rose, it tinted her pale skin with a dusky rose, as if she was lit inside from an internal fire. He drank it all down, the evidence of what he did to her. He would have missed all of it if he had not learned the lessons that she had taught him.

He would always be a selfish man. The gentleness she had taught him brought him pleasure.

But despite himself and the enjoyment he took in her arousal, the combination of things that they had talked about—that he had thought about—were too potent a cocktail for him to resist.

The possibility of making her pregnant had him so hard, he almost spilled in his pants just considering it. And the memory of how recently he had mated with her—both times—put him in touch again with those earlier emotions.

There were so many times when he had almost lost her, and she had almost lost him. Back in the beginning, when he had such dominant, possessive feelings, she could have rejected him out of hand, and that would have been it. She'd had every reason to reject him. He had chased her, terrorized her, and yet she still ending up loving him. Mating with him.

The mating frenzy always lay in the back of his mind, rather like a place that he had left, just around a corner. All he had to do was turn back, step around the corner, and he was there again.

Crazy from wanting her.

Insanely jealous of everything that took her attention away from him.

And needing her so badly, it felt like a knife in the gut.

After passing his hand over her hair, he lifted his head from the kiss. Tilting back her head, he pressed his lips against her vulnerable, beautiful neck.

He said against her fragile, petal soft skin, "You know how this goes, don't you?"

He had meant to take her back to the first time they had made love, when he had told her *I'm going to eat you until you scream.*

Instead, Pia grabbed his conversational gambit and skipped away with it.

"In a general sort of way," she whispered unsteadily. She ran her hands up his arms and dug her fingers into his shoulders. "You diddle here, I suck there. Or maybe you suck, and I diddle. Or both. Couple of pats, and ten or fifteen thrusts. 'Oh baby, you're so good, I can't take it,' *pow*, et cetera, 'let's go raid the fridge.'"

He felt his lips pull into a grin, and he made himself stop. Forcing some bite into his voice, he repeated, "*Ten* or *fifteen* thrusts?"

Her body shook as she started to giggle. "Well, you know, I never really counted them up. I'm usually too preoccupied with my own *pow* to keep track of what you're up to."

"Your *pow*," he growled. Her tank top was a pretty cherry red, one of his favorite colors. He eased the soft, thin material up her torso, and she lifted her arms so he could pull it over her head. "I think you're mistaken."

"About what?" Her laughing face emerged from underneath the top, hair disheveled and eyes sparkling.

She wasn't wearing a bra, and her breasts bounced free. Her beautiful, generously rounded breasts with the erect pink nipples. His mouth watered as he looked at them.

"That's *pows.* Plural," he told her. He cupped her breasts, massaging her nipples with his hands. His voice lowered into a growl. "You're too preoccupied with your multiple *pows* to keep track of what I'm doing. And I'm going to make you *pow* until you scream."

Her chuckle turned husky, and her eyes darkened with pleasure. She whispered, "Give it your best shot, big guy."

She hadn't called him that in months. A corner of his mouth lifted as he picked her up and dropped her on the bed.

Her eyes widened as she landed in a sprawl among suits and outfits. Her pale blond hair spilled over her face. Laughing, she started to roll away. "Clean clothes! Clean clothes!"

"Screw the clothes," he said. Bracing himself with one knee on the mattress of the bed, he picked handfuls of material up and tossed things aside.

Her laughter turned breathless. "I was going to pack all of that," she protested.

"Screw packing," he told her. As she tried to wiggle off the bed, he grabbed her by the hips and pulled her toward him.

"That's easy for you to say," she scolded, but there was no heat in her words. "You never pack your own stuff. Things just magically appear, clean and pressed, and ready whenever you need them."

She sat up, and her unsteady fingers caught the hem of his shirt and pulled it up his torso. He obliged her by pulling the shirt over his head and tossing it.

He picked up a handful of her hair, studying it. Pale gold strands gleamed in the late afternoon light. Obeying an impulse, he rubbed his face in the luxuriant mass. It felt like raw silk against his skin.

"Of course things magically appear when I need them," he told her. "That's why we have so much house staff."

She pulled back to glare at him. "Hey, I have news for you—all this prep work neatly laid out on the bed that you just threw on the floor? Your house staff had nothing to do with that. Your wife did."

His eyes narrowed on her. "We are both half naked on the bed, about to practice getting pregnant and giving each other multiple *pows*, and we're arguing about laundry?"

Her glare faded into uncertainty. After a pause, she said, "I guess so?"

Immensely satisfied, he nodded and pulled her up against his chest. They knelt there, skin against skin. Running his hands down the elegant curve of her back, he whispered against her mouth, "We are so married."

Her uncertainty vanished, to be replaced by happiness and heat, and a gleam of returning laughter. "Yes, we are, aren't we?"

"And twice mated," he whispered against her mouth. Her lips were plump and soft, and molded to his as he kissed her. "In case you were thinking about trying to get out of it."

"Well, technically, you're twice mated," she pointed out. "I didn't suffer amnesia, so I'm not."

His questing fingers found the fastening of her shorts. As he thumbed the fastening open and pulled the zipper down, he heard her breath catch.

"Don't give me semantics at a time like this, woman," he growled. "We're married, twice mated, and I'm about to get you barefoot and pregnant with my mighty sperm, so lie back and take your *pows*, will you?"

"Ooh." Her sexy little murmur of anticipation shot straight to his crotch.

As he eased her back, she went willingly, and when she was prone, she lifted her hips for him to yank off her shorts and undies. He tossed them as well without looking where they landed.

All his attention was fixed on the gorgeous woman lying in front of him, spread out like a feast. She glowed gently in the late afternoon sunlight, and he realized she had stripped away her dampening glamour so that she lay utterly naked for his perusal. Because her Wyr form was so rare, and it would be so incredibly dangerous for her if it ever became public, she hid her true nature from everybody but him, Liam, and the most trusted of their associates.

Warmth spread through him, pleasure and some kind of emotion he didn't know to put a name to. She gave him so much, before he ever thought to ask for it. She gave him everything.

He took off his jeans and lowered his body down over hers, watching her eyes darken as their nude bodies came flush against each other. When his rigid cock brushed against the graceful arc of her pelvic bone, he pulsed, and by the catch of her breath, he knew she had felt it too.

He reined in the impulse to cut loose. It was too soon, and she might not be ready for him. Growling under his breath from the buildup of internal pressure, he allowed himself to ravish her plump, inviting mouth, while with one hand, he roamed restlessly over the gentle curves of her body.

She twined her arms around him, kissing him with the same feverish need as he kissed her. The internal flames grew hotter, wilder. He cupped her breast, rolling her nipple between thumb and forefinger, while his tongue plunged deep into her mouth.

"You're burning up," she whispered against his lips.

"I'm on fire," he muttered.

Clear thinking disappeared in a haze of red. He bit down the soft skin of her slender throat, shifting his weight down so that he could suckle and tease her full breasts. Moaning, she moved restlessly under him. She held the back of his head with tense, shaking fingers, while the intoxicating scent of her arousal bloomed in the air.

His sucking bites brought the blood up under her glowing skin, so that the shadows of his touch clearly marked her.

He *loved* putting his mark on her. He *loved* that she fingered the places with evident enjoyment after they had made love. He knew her pleasure points, and he knew her limits, and the intimacy they had developed over the last eighteen months only enhanced their times together.

Moving farther down, he eased her long, slender legs over his shoulder so that she lay even more exposed to him. It was one of his favorite positions, and she shifted eagerly to accommodate him.

With the fingers from one hand, he parted the plump, pink petals of delicate flesh that surrounded her opening. Her earthy, rich scent filled his nostrils, and the sight of her was so exciting, his aching cock pulsed again.

Married. Twice mated.

Those human-inspired words were important, and immensely satisfying. They hinted at, but didn't touch the deepest essence of the truth between them.

But one word did. Finally, he put his mouth on her and growled against her most intimate flesh, "Mine."

DRAGOS'S GROWL VIBRATED through her lower body, and she started to shake in reaction. He was ferocity itself cloaked lightly in the guise of human flesh, but he had never once knowingly hurt her, and she knew he never would.

The sight of his dark head between her legs never failed to arouse her. Unerringly, his tongue found her clitoris, and he began to work her. The rhythm of his mouth pulsed throughout her body. It took over the beating of her heart and thudded in her veins.

Pleasure was a spiral, growing higher and tighter as he suckled her. When he worked two of his long, clever fingers into her tight passage, it blew through her like a supernova. He knew when the climax shook through her, and massaged her gently through it.

"My very first *pow* of the day," she whispered, stroking his hair.

His quick, gold gaze flashed to her. *Not your last one.* The sexy growl had taken over his mental voice. *Not by a long shot.*

Pure, languorous delight had her stretching in a luxurious, undulating roll. Thank the gods for a thorough, detail-oriented husband who was competitive even with himself.

All coherent thought blew out of her mind, as he suckled harder at her hypersensitive little nubbin of flesh. Having already peaked once, the pleasure came back stronger in a fierce wave of sensation. It cascaded along her nerve endings until the intensity became almost unbearable.

She couldn't keep her hips still. They rose up to meet his wise, relentless mouth. She tried to grab him by the hair, but he kept it too short, and the silken straight strands slipped through her fingers. The built-up tension was going to kill her if it didn't break soon. Her heart pounded like she was running, always running.

Always running toward him.

Her second climax slammed her back into the mattress. Flinging out her arms, she grabbed handfuls of the bedspread so that she could have something to hold on to in the maelstrom and coughed out a hoarse, breathless scream.

"Okay, okay," she panted, when she could formulate words. "Ease up now—Dragos, please . . ."

Not on your life, Mephistopheles purred in her head.

This time the peak of pleasure was immediate and savage, as if the dragon had taken her in his teeth and bodily shaken her.

Her legs clenched along his back, and another hoarse scream broke from her shaking lips. She swore at him, and her wicked lover laughed at her. Oh gods, everything inside of her was lit with fire, and he just wasn't . . . going . . . to . . . stop.

She tried to laugh too, but she had no breath. In desperation, she reached above her head for one of the pillows. She hit him over the head with it. "This isn't going to get me pregnant!"

At that, he rose up on his hands and knees and crawled up her body, at once so massive and liquid with power and grace, she lost what little breath she had.

From that angle, his chest looked immense, and his erection hung heavy and thick above his tight, round testicles. His gold eyes blazed with light and heat, and his expression had lost what little humanity it had.

"Oh, I'll get you pregnant," said the dragon in her face. "I'll fuck you until you can't walk."

"Promises," she tried to sneer. It came out more like a wheezing giggle. She hit him with the pillow again.

With a lightning fast move, he snatched it from her. Hooking an arm around her waist, he slid the pillow underneath her hips. She wiggled into place, tilting her pelvis up for him even as she reached for his cock with both greedy hands.

Together they positioned the broad, thick tip of his erection at her opening, and with one brutally efficient move, he thrust into her. He had lost his gentleness, and neither of them missed it. She was so slick and swollen, so sensitized, she came again as he ground himself against her. This time, she was past making any sound. She shook all over, and tears spilled out the corners of her eyes.

He destroyed her, completely. He tore away every barrier she had against the world, until he had conquered her at the core. Stripped and vulnerable, she did the only thing she could—she wound her arms around his neck and clung to him with everything she had.

He fucked her savagely, in short hard jabs, staring into her face with feral eyes. She was surrounded and filled with heat and pressure. He came in complete silence, thrust flush against her, his powerful body hard like iron. Her heavy eyelids drooped down as she felt him pulse inside of her.

As the pulsing slowed, she managed to unglue one of her shaking arms so that she could stroke his face, his hair. Gods, the love she felt for him was so intense sometimes it took her outside her own body.

Closing his incandescent eyes, he turned that feral, inhuman face into her caress and pressed his lips to her palm.

"How many thrusts was that?" His voice had gone guttural.

It took a moment for the meaning of his words to sink in. As wrecked she was, she burst out laughing weakly. "See? It's like I told you—I get so busy with my own *pows*, I don't pay any attention to what you're doing."

Breathing hard, he pulled out. Before she had a chance to make a disappointed face at his abrupt departure, he took her in a strong, unbreakable grip and flipped her so that she lay on her stomach, with the pillow still underneath her hips.

"Then don't mind me," he growled. "I'll carry on without you. Because I'm not done yet."

Not done yet.

The words ran down her spine in a liquid sizzle.

He had reached for the mating frenzy. Oh gods. It sent her muscles to shaking again, a deep, uncontrollable reaction.

Strength and energy flooded back into her limbs. She came up on her elbows. Tucking her knees in, she raised herself to him. It was one of the most primitive and enjoyable positions, and it satisfied something animalistic deep inside her.

Looking over her shoulder, she whispered, "I'm ready when you are, big guy. Let's go."

Like darkness eclipsing the moon, he came over her. It felt so right, so good as he penetrated her. It felt necessary. Closing her eyes, still shaking, she opened herself up and let her own mating frenzy come.

At one point, someone knocked on their door. When Dragos roared for them to go away, they did so, laughing. It was Eva.

Pia managed to pull herself together enough to say telepathically to the other woman, *Please feed Liam supper, and tell him Mommy and Daddy are very tired and will see him in the morning.*

Sure, I'll tell him, Eva said. *But you know he knows better, right?*

It's called polite fiction, Pia snapped. *That's what families tell each other, right?*

From down the hall, Eva laughed harder.

Pia was tempted to snap at her again, but just then Dragos did something to her to make her eyes roll back in her head, and the rest of the world faded away.

The rest of the evening and the night passed in a heated blaze, until finally exhaustion lay an inexorable claim on her and she fell asleep, draped bonelessly across Dragos's chest with his fists clenched in her hair.

Sometime later, much later, awareness brought her out of a deep sleep.

The first thing she noticed was that she was alone in bed, and every muscle ached. It was a good, deep ache that came from utter satiation.

Warm sunlight lay across one arm and shoulder.

Sunlight?

She managed to get one eye unglued. It revealed another bright, sunny day outside the nearby open balcony windows.

Sunlight never poured through those windows until late morning and early afternoon. They were so, so, so late, and she hadn't even packed yet.

"Oh, no," she muttered. It came out more like a croak.

"I've got to tell you, lover. That's not the most rousing thing you've ever said after a full night of lovemaking."

Dragos's voice came from across the room. With an immense effort, she turned her head and let it plop back down on the pillow.

Dragos lounged on a nearby chaise. He had showered although he hadn't shaved, and he had dressed in jeans while remaining shirtless and barefoot. Out of the corner of her eye, she saw that he had the bedroom TV turned to a news channel with the volume muted. He had his laptop on his lap, but as she watched, he set it aside.

"It's so late, and I haven't finished packing," she said. "What am I saying? I haven't even managed to sit upright yet."

One side of the bed dipped as he knelt on it to reach over to her. Pressing his mouth to her shoulder blade, he said against her skin, "I packed."

At the touch of his lips on her sensitive skin, heat coiled low in her body. She pushed it away, eyeing Dragos warily. "What do you mean, you packed?"

"I mean, I packed. Everything. My stuff, and your stuff." Running a flattened hand down her back, he nodded to the doorway.

She rose up on her elbows to look. All the suitcases were stacked by the door. "Makeup?"

"You had everything set on the counter."

She could hardly believe it. Dragos was the least domesticated person she knew. Scanning the floor, she found that it was bare of all the clothes he had tossed the previous night. "Toiletries?"

"Yes, your toiletries too. Don't look so skeptical. I watch what you do every day. I know what you use." His voice had deepened again as he kept stroking her back.

He loved to touch her, but late as it was, they couldn't afford to get lost in the mating frenzy again, or they would be two days late getting to D.C. and miss the White House thing altogether.

She reached for his hand, meaning to push him away, but somehow her fingers got tangled up with his instead.

Pulling his hand to her, she rested her cheek on it and mumbled, "Jewelry."

Even as she said it, she knew it was the most stupid of all her questions. Knowing him, he had probably packed the jewelry first, and only after he had gone through the case thoroughly in order to admire the jewels inside.

"You had your travel jewelry case out and ready to go," he said. "What do you think?"

The wide back of his strong hand had a sprinkle of black hair across the veins. She pressed a kiss to it. "I believe you."

"Everything is taken care of. All you need to do is shower and eat some breakfast, and then we can leave," he told her.

The thought of eating made her feel unexpectedly queasy. She pushed it aside as she sat up. "I'm not hungry, but I'd like a cup of coffee."

He nodded over to the chaise. When she looked in that direction again, she saw the tray sitting on the side table.

"You thought of everything." She smiled at him.

He didn't smile back. His gaze had dropped to her bare breasts, and his expression had turned sharp and predatory. Cupping a breast, he stroked his thumb along a darkened suck bruise.

He said in a low voice, "You know, we can always change our minds and go a day later."

The heat that shimmered between them felt volcanic and beat underneath her skin with a tribal tempo. Reaching hard for self-control, she covered his hand with hers. "And miss the kick off event for the summit at the White House tonight? Much as I would like to, you know we can't."

His black brows lowered. "We can."

The thing about the mating frenzy was, it had no sense. She smiled at him sidelong. "Or we can make love again on the plane."

His returning smile was quick and gleamed with anticipation. "Yes. Hurry up."

Chapter Three

PIA SHOWERED QUICKLY, and after wrapping the towel around her torso, she went into her closet to choose casual clothes for traveling—a comfortable pair of jeans, sandals, and a fitted, button-down shirt.

When she took the outfit to the bedroom, she found Dragos and their luggage already gone. While she had been in the shower, he had taken the news channel off mute and indulged in one of his bad habits by leaving the TV on.

It drove her crazy when he did that. She was congenitally incapable of leaving the room without turning off the TV first. As she shimmied into her jeans, she looked around the bedroom for the remote.

The news segment changed.

"Following on the heels of the terrible massacre in the Northern California Nightkind demesne this spring, Washingon DC is stepping up security for a week-long summit between the Elder Races demesne leaders and the human leaders of the U.S. government," the news caster said with a bright smile. "The recent upsurge in Elder Races violence over the last few years has made more than one human official pause, but the mass murder of ninety seven people—most of them human—by one of the Nightkind demesne's senior member of government has created a crisis for the Elder Races leaders that just won't go away. Federal lawmakers at the highest levels are calling for accountability for their actions, and all the Elder Races have responded . . ."

Which wasn't quite true.

Pia paused to glare at the image of the oblivious newscaster.

The truth was, federal lawmakers had called on the Nightkind demesne for an accounting of the multiple homicides, and the Nightkind regent Xavier del Torro had responded by suggesting the summit.

While the slaughter of so many people was quite horrible, over the last few months, her horror over what happened had turned to worried exasperation for how so many of the news channels insisted on making such a terrible crime sound like the Elder Races were murdering humans instead of reporting the more accurate story.

Which was that a dangerous, powerful, psychopathic Vampyre named Justine had killed all her attendants rather than risk letting any of them talk to her enemy, the Nightkind King Julian Regillus, and possibly leak valuable information about her whereabouts and activities. Or that Julian had personally seen that justice was done by hunting Justine down and killed both her and her co-conspirators.

But once the news had gotten skewed that way, other stories were highlighted—the damages in Chicago, when Dark Fae assassins attempted to kill Niniane, damages to various properties in San Francisco when Carling was a fugitive, and even the property damage in New York, caused by Dragos's roar when she had stolen his penny, were discussed over and over.

Skewed or not, they had a point.

They had a serious point.

And after watching the shit-storm that had hit the media in the aftermath of the Nightkind massacre, all the Elder Races leaders had agreed to the summit.

"But why does every newscast have to be an 'us against them' mentality?" she muttered. "Isn't it time to start talking about solutions instead of endlessly going over the problems?"

Finally locating the remote in the tousled bed covers, she clicked the off button forcefully, and peaceful silence flooded the room.

Yanking a hairbrush through her damp hair, she did a quick tour of the bathroom and their closets, but Dragos had been as good as his word and had packed everything.

In her closet, she paused at her jewelry cabinet. Then, after a few moment's thought, she opened it up.

What were the chances they might get pregnant? For the Elder Races in general, the chances were slim, and while they had been joking about Dragos's mighty sperm, the truth was both his nature and hers were so uniquely magical that there was no way to know how that might skew the general statistics.

Last time, she had gotten violently sick after they had been together only a few days. After all the brouhaha of finding out that she was indeed pregnant, and then her getting kidnapped, chased and almost killed, Dragos had given her a diamond pendant, infused with an anti-nausea spell, that had become her lifeline through the rest of her pregnancy. Predator and herbivore genes don't play together nicely in the womb.

And what if they were extraordinarily lucky and it did happen again?

After a few moments of hesitation, she pulled out the necklace, tucked it in its own velvet box, and thrust it into her purse. Better safe than sorry, because oh my lord, that nausea would make her one sorry Wyr, and if there was any week she couldn't afford to be sick, it was this one.

Satisfied with her decision, she went downstairs where Dragos was waiting.

They had given Liam options—he could either go to D.C. with them, or he could remain home to stay in school. Excited at joining the football team, he had elected to remain at home, although Dragos had kept him out of school that morning so they could say good-bye to him.

"No unexpected growth spurts," she told him, as she finger-combed his dark blond hair and straightened his collar. "And no sleepovers, so don't even bother asking. I want to Skype with you every day, so you can tell me how your day went."

"Yeah, okay." Grinning, he ducked away from her ministrations. "Come on, Mom, quit it. I'm all straight-ened up."

"Fine, I'm stopping. I love you." She grabbed his shoulders and hauled him close for a hug. Despite his complaints, his arms closed around her readily.

"Love you too," he muttered against her shoulder.

Public or open displays of affection had begun to embarrass him, which she thought was so darn adorable, because he still wanted to be hugged, but he had started to act sneaky about seeking out the hugs. She squeezed him tighter before she let him go.

"We're going to talk about a surprise for you when we get back," Dragos told him.

The puppy. She grinned. With everything that had happened, she had forgotten about that.

Liam perked up. "Oh yeah? What is it?"

"If I told you, it wouldn't be a surprise, would it?" Smiling, Dragos hooked a long arm around the boy and hauled him in for another hug. "Be good. And be careful out on the field."

At that, Liam sobered somewhat. He promised, "I will."

Over the summer, Dragos had commissioned an airstrip to be built just a mile away from their estate, so after their good-byes were said, the trip to the jet was short.

The security detail and house staff who would be covering the D.C. trip had already left around ten P.M. the night before, Dragos told her. That included Eva, while Hugh would remain at home to watch over Liam's welfare.

She did a happy little wiggle in her seat. That also

meant they would have the cabin of the jet to themselves. More sexy times were a-comin'.

In short order, they boarded the jet. The preflight checks had already been completed, so as soon as Andrew, one of the co-pilots, had tucked the luggage into compartments, closed the door and stepped into the cockpit, the engines began a high, powerful whine.

Pia had tucked her purse into a closet and thrown herself on one of the couches. As the plane started to roll down the runway, Dragos turned to her.

The somewhat terse expression he had worn around other people vaporized. He looked feral again, and clenched.

Her body knew that look. All he had to do was look at her like that, and reach for her with those two big hands, and desire flooded her in a liquid gush of heat.

Either the airplane's acceleration, or Dragos's insistence, pushed her back against the leather cushions. She melted back willingly, while he tore her clothes off. Material ripped—she didn't know what got damaged—she might have to pull out one of her suitcases to get something else she could wear later. . . .

Then all coherent thought vanished. After he finished tearing off her clothes, he stripped rapidly. The slanting light from the windows striped his powerful body. Heavy muscles rippled under dark bronze skin as he came between her legs. The hunger that gripped her was insatiable. She ran her hands over sleek dark hair that covered the wide expanse of his chest.

When he fingered her and found her ready, he entered her without ceremony. Gasping, she threw her head back at the intimate invasion. Thunderous noise vibrated all around her, accompanied by Dragos's low, animalistic growl reverberating against her torso.

Sometimes she didn't know herself when she was with him. She lost that much control. They coupled wildly together. The couch wasn't big enough to contain them.

At one point, Dragos pulled them to the floor so that he could hold her ankles wide as he fucked her. She reached for anything she could grasp to brace herself at the onslaught, while the unbearably intense pleasure shot straight into the stratosphere, higher than the plane, until she shattered with waves of completion.

The rest of the trip disappeared in a passionate haze. He took her again, standing and bracing himself with one hand against the wall, while she wrapped her legs around his waist and hung on for dear life.

Then the air pressure changed slightly, signifying descent, and the pilot's voice came over the intercom. "Just wanted to check in to let you know we'll be landing in twenty minutes. It's a beautiful day in D.C. and unseasonably warm for October, a balmy 78 degrees and sunny. Looks like you'll have good weather for the week."

Dragos lifted his head from her shoulder. They were both sweaty, and his black hair looked even darker when damp.

She had started out the day by oversleeping, and now she had no strength in any of her limbs. She whimpered,

"We have to be presentable in twenty minutes?"

Bending his head, he kissed her swiftly. "They'll remain in the cockpit until I tell them they can come out."

That would mean they would be sitting in the cockpit, knowing full well what she and Dragos had been doing in the cabin.

But who was she trying to fool? Their sex scent drenched the cabin air. Even if she rushed, as soon as the pilots stepped out, they would know what had happened.

She rubbed her face. Her skin felt abraded by his whiskers. "Fine," she muttered. "I get to shower first." If they were anywhere but on the plane, she would suggest that they shower together, but the shower, while luxurious for a jet, was too small to accommodate both of them at once.

He cocked an eyebrow at her. "Are you sure about that? You don't look capable of moving."

He sounded immensely satisfied with that fact. Bah, men. She tried to scowl at him. "Yes, I'm sure. You're faster in the shower than I am. I have more hair to get clean than you do. Besides, if we're not done by the time we land, I would rather they scented you, not me."

His satisfied expression disappeared, and he scowled back. Clearly he didn't like that thought either, even though their pilots were a mated pair of male Wyr ravens and wouldn't be interested in Pia anyway. The dragon was an exceedingly jealous creature.

Standing, he scooped her into his arms and carried her to the back, into the luxurious bathroom. Then he set her on her feet again. He told her, "I'll get your clothes. Hurry up."

She chuckled and stepped into the cubicle for her second shower of the day. Hot water ran soothingly over tired, abused muscles, and while she wanted to stand there and soak it in, she forced herself to lather and rinse quickly, so Dragos could have the shower while she dressed.

The jet's descent steepened as she inspected her clothes. It was her panties that had torn. She didn't have time to dig out a new pair, so she stuffed them in the trash bin and dressed without them, then dug out a travel hairbrush from the stock of toiletries in the bathroom and yanked it through her wet, unruly hair. That was going to have to do. The pilots would still know what happened, of course, but it wouldn't feel as exposing as having them scent it on her skin.

As she sat on the toilet to slip on her sandals, Dragos sluiced off within two minutes, dressed with quick economy and ran long fingers through his wet hair. Then together, they stepped back into the cabin and took their seats just moments before the plane touched ground.

As they braked hard, she felt queasy again, but over the last several hours, she had put out an extraordinary amount of energy. She was sore, achy and tired, and she'd only drunk a cup of coffee for breakfast.

It was far too soon to feel any effects from possibly getting pregnant. The queasiness had to be a touch of motion sickness on an empty stomach.

Still, she couldn't stop herself from placing a hand

low on her flat stomach and turning her focus inward to search for a tiny, new precious spark of life.

There was none.

She knew that. She *knew* better, but still a leaden disappointment pulled her down.

Dragos's massive, powerful hand came over hers, warming her. He pressed gently. She opened her eyes. She didn't know what her face revealed, but his expression gentled. He put an arm around her, and she leaned against him, resting her head on his shoulder as the plane taxied to a stop.

The cabin door opened. Dragos's gentle expression faded as both pilots stepped out, but they kept their faces polite and indifferent, and exercised terrific discretion. As his mate pulled pieces of luggage from the bins, Andrew said cheerfully, "Welcome to D.C. I hope you have a great stay."

"Good flight," said Dragos. "For a plane."

"Thanks," Andrew said, with a quick, understanding grin.

When Dragos stood, Pia did too.

Her slight queasiness took a sharp turn for the worst.

"Excuse me," she muttered, bolting for the back of the plane and the bathroom, and slamming the door shut.

She barely made it to the toilet before she vomited violently. Clutching the rim, her eyes streamed as her body heaved.

What. The. Hell.

"Pia." Dragos's sharp voice sounded just outside.

The door rattled. "You locked the door. What's wrong?"

He hated locked doors between them. But this time he was going to have to suck it up. There were times when you just needed a moment or two by yourself, damn it.

"Nothing," she gritted out. "I'll be out in a sec."

She grabbed a tissue and mopped her damp face while she waited to see if she was done.

After an uncertain lurch, her stomach seemed to let go of its hissy fit and settled. She climbed to her feet on shaky legs, flushed and compulsively checked again for a life spark.

Nothing. Of course, nothing. Looking grimly at her reflection in the mirror, she shook her head at her own foolishness.

The door rattled again. Dragos said telepathically, *If you don't open this door in the next sixty seconds, I'll come through it.*

She disappeared for TWO SECONDS, and suddenly he was completely determined to break the plane. She rolled her eyes.

No reason to break down the door, she said testily. *I had a touch of tummy trouble and had to use the toilet. I'm just washing up now.*

All of that was true, if a bit ambiguous. She washed her hands and face, and opened a travel packet of mouthwash to rinse out her mouth.

The door rattling stopped.

"Okay," said Dragos. "Do you want your purse?"

Now that she had given him some reassurance, he

sounded perfectly mild and sane. Ha. She had gotten to know him all too well, and that perfectly mild and sane voice of his wasn't going to fool her ever again.

She told him, "Yes, please."

Now that the plane was on the tarmac and no longer moving—and her stomach was completely empty—she actually did feel better.

She squared her shoulders and opened the bathroom door. Dragos leaned against one of the seats, waiting for her. He handed the purse to her, while his sharp gaze ran down her body.

She sighed. "It's not a big deal. The only thing I've put in my stomach since lunch yesterday was coffee."

"We'll rectify that as soon as we get to the Wyr residence." Straightening, he nodded to the two pilots waiting near the head of the plane. "Have a good week. I'll be in touch when we finalize a time for our departure."

"Very good, sir," said Andrew.

Putting that rather ignominious arrival firmly behind her, she followed Dragos as he strolled down the aisle, and they deplaned into the sunny day.

EVA WAS WAITING for them in the pickup lane, leaning against an armored black Cadillac Escalade.

Preferring to drive, Dragos took the keys and slid into the driver's seat, while Pia got into the front passenger seat and Eva climbed in the back.

Actually, he would have preferred to avoid the heavy D.C. traffic altogether and fly directly to the Wyr residence, but there were strict no-fly laws over the area where they were headed. His cloaking ability was excellent, but he wasn't altogether sure what the human sensors could detect of his presence.

Prosaic radar technology couldn't detect him when he was cloaking, but he would bet the Cuelebre Enterprises gross profit for the year on humans having more than just mechanical sensors guarding their capital. If he were a human in charge of guarding such an important city, he would have squadrons of witches laying protection spells over the city like gigantic, invisible spiderwebs.

In any case, now was also not the time to break human laws and get everybody riled over something relatively unimportant. Not when humankind had become so nervous at the perceived damages caused by the Elder Races in the last two years.

The Elder Races held a lot of magical Power, the most in the world. But humans held a lot of power of a different sort, in terms of sheer numbers in their population, along with military strength. Over the last few centuries, their numbers had multiplied so that their presence virtually covered the earth.

Continuing to coexist was the very best thing that could happen for everybody concerned. If they couldn't achieve amicable coexistence . . .

Well, the world would get a lot colder and meaner, if that happened. The possibility troubled him more than he liked to say.

So he throttled back his impatience, put the car in drive and pulled sedately away from the curb and into traffic.

"Tell the house staff to prepare a meal for when we arrive," he said over his shoulder.

"You got it," Eva said.

He glanced in the rearview mirror. Eva's dark head bent as she texted on her phone. His attention turned to Pia, who watched out her window curiously. She had never been to D.C. before and was hoping to find time to sightsee some of the famous landmarks.

Did she look more pale than usual? She wasn't wearing makeup. Frowning, he asked telepathically, *You okay?*

She turned to smile at him. *Don't fuss. I'm fine.*

Fuss? He wasn't a fusser. Scowling, he accelerated aggressively to cut across traffic to the fast lane. After he finished the maneuver, he told her shortly, *You look pale.*

I always look pale. She placed a slender hand on his thigh. Her light touch managed to dispel his bad temper. She said aloud, "How long do we have until we need to leave for the White House this evening?"

"Couple hours." He glanced at her again, noting the dark shadows underneath her eyes. "There's time to eat, and you can take a nap before we go."

She shook her head at him with a smile filled with feminine pity. "Oh no, I can't. I've never been to the White House before. I'm not going to just throw on clean clothes and run my fingers through my hair, like you do."

One corner of his mouth lifted. "Well, at some point I am going to shave too."

Her eyes danced. "So am I. Plus, there's the makeup, and I'm going to put my hair up, so I need to allow time for hot curlers."

He loved it when she pinned her hair up in big, fat curls, in a style reminiscent of sixties chic. It bared the elegant line of her neck, which he loved to explore with his mouth.

Later, when it was time to take her hair down, he would be the one to do the small chore, letting the curls fall loose one by one as he kissed the nape of her neck and slid down the zipper of her dress.

In an instant, he was hard again and aching for her. It was hard to believe he had just taken her so many times on the plane. The mating frenzy was the only thing that had ever held him in its grip for long.

If it was a prison, it was one he didn't want to leave. He relished its claws digging underneath his skin, driving him to extremes. But they wouldn't have time now to succumb to another bout of lovemaking until after the evening's function.

Forcing the urge back, he exhaled on a long, steady breath.

Pia's fingers tightened on his thigh. Either she could scent the mating pheromones, or she had been eyeing his crotch.

He looked at her. Her gaze was down and directed sidelong. She *was* watching his crotch, and a rose blush stained her pale cheeks. She raised her gaze to look at him, biting her lip. She was as much a prisoner of the mating frenzy as he was, and she looked helpless with desire.

Fuck yeah.

He loved it when she was helpless and begging for his touch.

"Jeebus," muttered Eva. "Gettin' hot in here." She rolled down her window and fresh air swirled into the car. "Thank the gods we're almost there."

In short order, he turned onto Massachusetts Avenue. He glanced at Pia again as they approached the section known as Embassy Row, where embassies, diplomatic missions and other representations were concentrated.

The mansions grew larger, older and grander, and the rows of town houses became more spacious. When he pulled through the front gates of the Wyr mansion, her eyes went round.

She whispered, "This is ours?"

"This is ours," he said. "It's been the Wyr residence in Washington since 1895."

As he parked under the portico, the front doors opened, and two uniformed Wyr came briskly down the steps. Behind them, the gates quietly closed.

She unbuckled her seat belt as she craned to stare up at the roof, as she asked, "How many rooms does it have?

"Eight bedrooms, twelve bathrooms, all modernized," he told her. "Dining room, library, etc."

"Along with a very modern home theater, bowling

alley, and a wine cellar in the basement," Eva added. "There's a black, wrought iron railing that runs up both sides of a marble staircase. You should see the house lit up at night. I took a walk through the neighborhood last night. It's all white marble and light. Very elegant."

The property also had tunnels that ran several blocks underground in different directions before leading to innocuous-looking openings—street gutters, the sewage system with manholes and the like.

Nobody would trap the Wyr in this place. In case of emergency, those who couldn't fly could still get out. He always liked to lay contingency plans, especially in places that could be less than friendly.

Once the car had stopped moving, Eva stepped out to direct the guards to the rear of the SUV, where they pulled out luggage and carried it inside.

Pia squinted at Dragos. "You almost never come here. It's got to be a hellacious expense to keep this property maintained."

He inclined his head in agreement. "When I come here, I come as a world-class power. Washington does well to remember that. One of the ways I choose to remind them of that fact is by maintaining this residence."

"I guess keeping one of the town houses wouldn't carry the same impact, even though I'm sure they're just as spectacular in their own way."

"Also, I would never share walls with someone else. It leaves one too vulnerable." He stepped out of the vehicle, his sharp predator's gaze studying the surroundings outside the black iron fence.

He knew watchers were stationed on the residence, both human and other. He might have carefully cultivated allies among humankind, but he had no true friends here. Humankind was as wary of the dragon as any of the Elder Races. Many of the watchers would be unfriendly, but none of them were visible.

As he surveyed the area, the guards returned to make sure they had carried everything in. One of the guards, a tall, young handsome male, offered his hand to Pia with a smile.

Violent jealousy shot through Dragos's body. Moving fast, he rounded the front of the vehicle and bared his teeth to hiss at the other male before Pia had a chance to grasp the outstretched fingers.

The guard recoiled, turning pale, and Pia's expression stilled as her gaze turned sharp and wary. She paused, one slender, sandaled foot already on the pavement.

Dragos drew in a deep breath and fought for calm. He said quietly to the guard, "Go into the house."

Bowing his head, the guard fled, leaving him and Pia to regard each other.

Finally he said, "You don't have to say anything. I know that was excessive."

"Are you all right?" she asked.

Was he? She had asked the question in all seriousness, so he pondered that. "I think so. Just—be careful not to get too close to any other males right now. I'm too much in touch with the mating frenzy."

"I understand," she said quietly. "Perhaps we should

have considered things more carefully and put off trying to get pregnant until after this week was over."

"We made an emotional decision. There's nothing wrong with that. We'll make it work. I'll talk to Bayne, so he can warn the staff, and I'll be on guard when we're in public." He bent slightly to extend his hand to her. "Welcome to one of your homes, Lady Cuelebre."

The concept that she was part owner of the magnificent mansion clearly startled her, as her eyes widened even further, but she swallowed down whatever she might have said and placed her hand in his.

As he supported Pia's exit out of the Cadillac and straightened, he swept the scene once more.

Then Dragos Cuelebre, Lord of the Wyr, escorted his mate and wife into his Washington abode.

Chapter Four

ONCE INSIDE THE elegant foyer, Pia told Eva, "I want to see everything."

Dragos tightened his hold on her fingers. "You need to eat."

"Ten minutes," she said. "I want the quick tour. I'll be right back."

Her eyes were sparkling and the color was back in her cheeks, so he reluctantly let her go. As the two women jogged up the marble staircase, Bayne appeared, strolling down the hallway.

As the sentinel on duty for the week, Bayne was in charge of all the security details. Instead of wearing his usual jeans, T-shirts and boots, which was the standard attire for all the sentinels at home in New York, the gryphon wore a dark gray suit, with a black shirt and tie. The outfit emphasized his large, tall build and short, tawny hair.

Dragos ran a critical eye down the other man's figure. The excellent cut of the suit hid his weapons well. Bayne would be an acceptable addition at any except the most formal functions, and for those, he had brought a black tux.

As the other man reached him, Bayne gave him a nod in greeting. “One of my guards wanted me to apologize to you on his behalf,” the sentinel said, tucking his hands into the pockets of his tailored slacks. “Rather profusely, I might add. So, he’s really, really sorry. What’d he do?”

Dragos blew out a breath through his nostrils in an inaudible growl. It was going to be a long damn week. “He almost took Pia’s hand to help her out of the car, and I snapped at him.”

“I see.” Bayne’s tone was neutral.

He shot the other man a look from under lowered brows. “Pia can get out of a fucking car by herself. She doesn’t need males tripping over themselves to touch her. And in any case, I’ll be the one to escort her. At all times. You hear?”

Eyebrows raised, Bayne pursed his lips and nodded. “Yeah, I hear you. I also sense there may be some, ah, underlying tension?”

Dragos strode for the dining room, and the other man fell into step beside him. Telepathically, he said, *Keep this confidential. We’re trying to get pregnant, and yes, it’s brought back the mating frenzy. So, make sure everyone is warned.*

Bayne began to smile. *And I was worried this week might be boring. I’ll prep everybody to take care.*

In the dining room, the long, gleaming antique mahogany table had two place settings at one end.

They lived very informal lives in upstate New York. Even when they stayed in the penthouse in Cuelebre Tower in the city, more often than not, Pia chose to cook. But here in D.C., appearances were everything. He noted in approval the gleaming polished silver, formal bone china, and heavy cream linen napkins.

Two uniformed staff were in the process of bringing dishes of hot food from the kitchen—pasta with sun-dried tomatoes and garlic in olive oil, a kale and artichoke salad, ham sliced fresh off the bone, roasted potatoes, and green beans garnished with something colorful and red, perhaps peppers.

"Set another place at the table," Dragos told one of the servers. She nodded and headed back into the kitchen. He said to Bayne, "Stay and eat with us. I want to hear about everything you've been doing and what you've heard so far."

"You got it."

"Make that two places," Pia said to the server from the doorway.

She and Eva walked into the room. At first Pia made as if she might go to hug Bayne—something that was perfectly acceptable under normal circumstances, and very like her usual affectionate style with all the sentinels—but Bayne took a nimble step back, and she jerked to a halt and redirected to pick up one of the place settings.

It could have been ridiculously uncomfortable, but dancing around sensitive mating issues was such a way of life for the Wyr, everybody adjusted smoothly, and within a few moments, they were all seated at the table and serving themselves from the silver platters of food.

"Almost all the other demesne leaders have already

arrived," Bayne said, as he piled ham onto his plate.

All of the U.S. demesnes had committed to coming—Tatiana, the Light Fae Queen from Los Angeles; Ferion, the new Elven High Lord from Charleston; Dragos, as leader of the Wyr in New York; Isalynn, the head of the witches demesne from Kentucky; Jered, the current head of the Demonkind assembly from Houston; and even Niniane, the Dark Fae Queen from Chicago, had come, despite the fact she spent most of her time in the Dark Fae Other land Adriyel.

Dragos shook his head. All the demesne leaders convening in D.C. at the same time. That had never happened before. To anyone paying attention, that alone said more than anything else about how seriously the demesnes were taking the human unrest.

He asked, "Did Julian come?"

"Well no, not Julian," Bayne replied. "He's still adamant about taking a year off from the political scene, but Xavier is here as Julian's regent and Nightkind representative. From what I heard, Isalynn was arriving sometime this afternoon too. Tric—Niniane and Tiago got in last night. Eva and I had dinner with them."

"We ordered a shit ton of pepperoni pizza," Eva said with a grin.

Pia's tired face lit with pleasure. "I'm looking forward to seeing them. How are they?"

"Really well," Bayne told her. "All the fresh air and potential assassinations in Adriyel are good for Tiago. And Niniane looks happy. Only it's more than that."

"How so?" Dragos asked curiously.

Bayne frowned. "I guess I want to say she looks settled."

"I'm so glad to hear that." Pia smiled.

Bayne helped himself to another slice of ham. "The not-so-good news—there are thousands of people outside the White House, protesting the summit. It's been all over the news. There's been backlash to that as well on the news, with some idiots on the other side putting down the human protestors for being close-minded bigots." The sentinel looked at Pia. "I know you were looking forward to doing some sightseeing if you could find any time, but I don't recommend it. Not for this trip."

The pleasure died from Pia's expression, and she looked tired and pale again. She said quietly, "Of course, that doesn't matter."

It did matter. Anything that drained the smile from her face mattered. Likely nothing dangerous would happen in any potential sightseeing jaunt, but there could be some unpleasantness.

Dragos told her, "Civil unrest happens all the time. Look at the sixties and the Vietnam War. We'll come back when things have calmed down. I'll take you sightseeing, myself."

"I'd like that," she told him. Abruptly, she set aside her cutlery. "If you'll excuse me, I'm going to go get ready for the evening."

He glanced at her plate. She had eaten perhaps half of her food.

Eva stood too. "I'll check to see if they're done ironing your dress and bring it up if they are."

"Thanks." Pia stepped close to press a kiss to Dragos's forehead. She told him telepathically, *I ate what I wanted. Don't fuss.*

I don't fuss, goddammit, he growled.

She chuckled in his head as she walked away. *Keep telling that to yourself, my love.*

He glowered at her plate but didn't say another word.

BREATHING EVENLY, PIA climbed the magnificent staircase on shaky legs.

She managed to get to the bathroom in the master suite before she began vomiting. Rushing to the bathroom sink instead of the toilet, because it was closer, she made it just in time before her body struggled to rid itself of everything she had just put in her stomach.

When she finished, she hung her head, panting, while she tried to think.

I'm usually healthy as a horse.

(Heh. Horse.)

Why would I start vomiting now, of all times? The timing seems awfully suspicious.

Putting her hand to her abdomen, she sent her awareness into her body again. This time, she wasn't distracted by the jet landing. She didn't do just a cursory scan, but went deeper than she had before.

No life spark. Not even the tiniest, newest hint of a little spark.

Unwelcome tears filled her eyes. It was stupid to feel such disappointment. She needed to find some emotional ballast. They had barely started to try to get pregnant. Realistically, it could take them a very long time before they either got pregnant or eventually gave up.

And she was okay with that, except . . . why was she shaky and vomiting all of a sudden?

"I can't get sick," she muttered. "Not now of all times. This trip is too important."

Let alone the question of what was making her sick. She didn't get colds. She rarely, if ever, caught the flu, and anyway, flu season had barely started. It was far more likely for her to break a limb than to come down with some kind of illness.

Glancing at the sink had her stomach lurching again. Quickly, she turned on the water to rinse out the basin as footsteps sounded in the bedroom.

Eva called out, "I've got the dress."

"Great," she said, watching the water swirl away the last of the evidence.

"You sound so thrilled," Eva told her dryly. Pia hadn't had a chance to close the bathroom door, so Eva appeared in the open doorway. The other woman frowned. "What's wrong?"

Straightening from the sink, Pia wiped her mouth as she replied, "What makes you think something is wrong?"

Eva's dark gaze narrowed. "Because you look like shit."

Eva was utterly devoted to her, and completely loyal,

except, Pia knew, in one instance. If Eva thought something was wrong with Pia, she would tell Dragos in a heartbeat, despite what Pia might have to say about it.

And if Dragos thought for a second that something was wrong, he would overreact.

He would ditch the summit and fly her personally back to New York to a whole herd of Wyr doctors.

But despite what Dragos said about civil unrest, this summit was too important to ditch. People protested any number of things, yet this issue had infiltrated the U.S. government. Lawmakers were unsettled, and that meant the worst kind of trouble if they couldn't repair relations.

Pia wasn't exactly sure what the worst kind of trouble would mean. Her imagination wasn't good enough to create something that seemed dire enough, but she did know the schism would be felt across the entire country and throughout the rest of the world.

What was a bout or two of vomiting in the face of something like that?

So she lied. Well, misdirected, at least.

"I was up all night having crazy monkey sex," she said, turning away from Eva's too-sharp gaze to go back into the bedroom and look for her purse. "Of course I look like shit. That's why I'm going to slap ten pounds of makeup on my face after I take a shower."

Eva shrugged. "Okay. Need anything else?"

"No thanks, you can go get ready now." With Dragos so touchy at the moment, Eva was not just Pia's main bodyguard but probably her only one for the week. "See you downstairs."

As Eva left, she pulled the door closed behind her, and Pia was finally alone. She located her purse, tucked on a table by a large vase filled with purple irises and yellow roses, and pulled out the jewelry box holding the diamond pendant.

She didn't have time to be sick, but luckily she had something she could do about it for now. If she was still sick later, she would see a doctor next week when she got home.

As soon as she settled the necklace into place around her neck, she felt better, steadier. That'd do.

With a renewed sense of purpose, she turned back to the bathroom. Now it was time to get down to business.

By the time Dragos stepped into the bedroom, she had showered, dried her hair and rolled it up in hot curlers, and she sat at a vanity in a royal blue dressing gown as she applied the requisite ten pounds of makeup.

He walked over to her, hooked a finger into the neckline of the dressing gown and pulled it away so that he could kiss her naked shoulder. At the touch of his warm, firm mouth on her skin, a shiver of pleasure ran down her spine, and she leaned back against his thighs with a throaty murmur. She had to make a conscious effort to remember to hold on to her mascara wand as he cupped her breast.

"We don't have time for that," she told him.

"I know," he murmured, massaging her through the thin silk. "I just couldn't help touching you." He grew still. Then his hand left her breast to touch the diamond pendant as his gold gaze met hers in the mirror.

"No, I'm not," she told him in answer to the question he hadn't asked. "I'm wearing it as a precaution. You know, just in case. I don't want to throw up unexpectedly on anybody important this week. Besides, it's pretty."

His hard mouth pulled into a slow, sexy smile. He touched the diamond where it dangled just above the hollow of her breasts. "It is pretty, isn't it? And it's resting in one of my very favorite places in the world. I look forward to taking it off later this evening."

She looked forward to taking it off later too, but for an entirely different reason. Hopefully by that point the strange bout of sickness would have passed and she would be back to normal.

Careful not to mess either her curling hair or her makeup, she turned her head to press a kiss against his forearm. His hand traveled up to caress the line of her neck. "What are you wearing this evening?"

"I decided to go ultrachic," she said. "So I settled on the black sheath Dior."

"Perfect." He smiled. "I'd better shower and shave, and we'll leave in a half an hour. Is that enough time for you to finish getting ready?"

"Absolutely. All I have to do is take the curlers out, pin up my hair and slip on the dress." She turned her attention back to her reflection and picked up her lipstick. Around the *O* she made with her lips, she said, "Oh, and also do this."

He murmured, "You look good enough to eat."

"Don't you dare," she warned. "You'll mess everything up, and I don't have time to pull this off again."

Laughing, he stripped off his clothes. "Oh, I dare. I'll just eat you later."

Nude, he walked into the bathroom, and she had to pause to admire his powerful, lithe body. His sleek, heavy muscles rippled under dark bronze skin. In his human form or as a dragon, he was the most magnificent male she had ever laid eyes on.

She raised her voice. "I thought you should know. You make me so stinking happy. Especially when you walk around nude."

His laughter sounded. "You make me pretty stinking happy too, lover."

The sound of the shower started, and only then was she able to turn back to what she was doing.

She triple-checked her makeup for any flaws. By the time she had shimmied into the floor length, strapless gown and slipped on her high heeled Pradas, Dragos's electric travel shaver was buzzing in the bathroom. Quickly she pulled out the hot curlers and ran her fingers through her hair. Large shining curls tumbled around her bare shoulders.

The buzz of his razor stopped. She looked over her shoulder and found him frozen in the doorway. Except for a towel slung around his hips, he was still nude, and he stared at her with such naked hunger, it scorched her skin.

"I think I've changed my mind. I'll leave my hair down tonight." Tilting her head, she gave him a small smile. "Our half an hour is almost up. Shouldn't you be hurrying?"

His sharp intake of breath was audible across the room. She laughed. Stepping back, he slammed the bathroom door.

When he stepped out again, five minutes later, he was fully dressed. Fastening the last of her diamond stud earrings into her ear, she turned away from the vanity mirror and lost the ability to breathe.

She could almost get used to the daily reality of how he impacted her—almost—until she saw him like this, his massive, powerful body clothed in a severe, elegant black tux. The formal clothes did nothing to make him appear domesticated. If anything, they highlighted his handsome, brutal features, jet-black hair and piercing gold eyes, while the pristine white shirt brought out the richness of his dark bronze skin.

His soft growl reached her from across the room. "Don't look at me like that, or we really won't get out the door this evening."

She jerked away and scooped up her beaded black clutch. Like a gawky yearling with too much leg, she didn't feel quite in control of all her limbs. "Right," she muttered. "Out the door."

Quiet masculine laughter ghosted through her head. He strode for the door and held it open for her. Somehow she managed to walk out of the bedroom.

They made it downstairs with three minutes to spare of the half hour Dragos had given her. Bayne and Eva were waiting for them in the front hall. Bayne wore a tux too, his evening clothes heightening his rugged good looks, while Eva wore a silk gray Chanel suit.

"I still think you should have worn the red dress," Pia told her. "You look stunning in red."

The other woman shook her head with a grin. "Not while I'm on duty. The heels that go with that red dress are killer to run in."

"All set?" Bayne asked Dragos.

Dragos nodded, and the four of them stepped outside where two black SUVs and a limousine were waiting. Security rode in the SUVs in front and behind, while Bayne and Eva climbed with Dragos and Pia into the back of the limo.

At first their conversation remained lighthearted. Dragos took her hand, lacing long, dark fingers through hers while Bayne and Eva engaged in good-natured banter.

As Pia listened to them with a smile, she absentmindedly scratched at her right thigh. She hadn't taken the time to smooth lotion on after her shower, and her skin felt dry and itchy.

The banter died away, and Bayne and Eva fell silent as they drew close to the White House.

Protestors lined the street, carrying signs and shouting at the passing cavalcades. Pia watched the faces scroll past. The armored limo blocked the sounds so she couldn't hear what the protestors were shouting, but their expressions were angry and distorted.

Disquieted and scratching at her itchy thigh again, she glanced at Dragos. He was wearing his inscrutable expression, his gold gaze flat and unrevealing as he watched the protestors. It was one of his most dangerous expressions.

What was he thinking when he looked into the crowd? With a single pass over their heads and a rain of dragon fire, he could so easily destroy all of them.

Of course, that would mean he would also destroy the entire Wyr way of life as well.

She crooned in his head, *Honey, I'm so proud of you for not killing anybody.*

His gaze flashed to hers, and that flat, assessing expression vanished as he laughed. Squeezing her fingers, he told her, *Week's not over yet.*

More seriously, she asked, *What do you think it will take to smooth things over?*

His sexy mouth took on a cynical twist. *Money, business and political agreements, the promise of less violence from the Elder Races, and a lot of charm. Other people, like you, are going to have to supply the charm.*

She nodded, unsurprised by that last bit. *If I'm expected to dance with anybody, you're going to have to suck in your mating crazy. You up for that?*

The laughter left his face, and he gave her a sour look. *I'll make it happen. Thankfully, most human male politicians are old, ugly, lying fuckers. They're not your type at all.*

It was her turn to burst out laughing. *Well, you are old, and you do lie better than anybody I know.*

His eyelids lowered. *That might be so, but you don't think I'm an ugly fucker.*

True. She laughed harder. He might deal with politics out of necessity, but at his core, Dragos was far too rude to make an excellent politician. His real skills lay in cutthroat business.

And war. He was unsettlingly talented at going to war.

That thought sobered her up fast. Still absently rubbing at her thigh, she looked out the window again as they passed through the security gates and approached the White House.

When the limo rolled to a smooth stop, Bayne and Eva exited first, then Dragos.

Camera lights flashed nearby, blinding her as she took Dragos's hand and stepped out of the vehicle. She looked up at the famous, imposing building. At first she had thought she would be very nervous at facing the evening, but to her surprise, a sense of calm anticipation settled over her.

Time to go make nice with the old, ugly, lying fuckers.

Giving Dragos a sidelong, laughing glance, she tucked her arm into the crook of his sleeve and walked with him into the building.

Chapter Five

THE WHITE HOUSE function was a large, lavish affair. Ostensibly, the purpose was to give all the senators and members of Congress a chance to mingle with the seven demesne leaders as a way to break the ice for the week's meetings and help to dissipate interracial tensions.

Dragos had never told anyone what happened in his head when he entered such large gatherings, not even Pia.

The dragon rose up to look out of his human-seeming eyes.

Look at all the fragile humans, dressed in their finery and girded with a sense of their own importance. He took note of the glittering jewels that the women wore, the beat of pulses at soft, vulnerable throats, and the way eyes slid away from meeting his.

The president and first lady greeted them with polite smiles. Silently, Dragos inclined his head when spoken to, while the dragon thought, I play at your games because it suits me to do so.

President Ben Johnson was a hardy, athletic-looking male in his early sixties, and universally acknowledged to be a charming, poised and intelligent man, but when he spoke, all the dragon heard was bleating, like a sheep. His mate responded with a quick reply, and both president and first lady smiled at her.

The pleasantries over, the dragon and his mate moved away to greet other dignitaries. Frailer, self-important prey.

They came face-to-face with an enemy—the vice president of the United States, Sarah Colton—and her husband, Victor. The vice president was much younger than the president. A graduate of the Yale law program, she was a clever, trim brunette in her early forties with a photogenic smile.

Dragos whispered in Pia's head, *Vice President Colton is one of the ones responsible for stirring up much of the anti-Elder Races sentiment in Congress. Along with Senator Jackson, she spearheaded setting up the federal subcommittee that is investigating alleged abuses of power by the Elder Races.*

Pia's smile never wavered. She had grown used to their internal dialogue at such functions. *Senator Jackson—he's the one who lost his son in a boating accident earlier this year, right? I remember when news of his death was splashed all over the news.*

Yes.

This time no pleasantries, no matter how insincere, were exchanged. Neither the vice president nor her husband offered to shake hands. Dragos did not deign to offer his either, and with a quick glance sideways at him, Pia took her cue and remained self-contained and composed.

"Mr. Cuelebre," said the vice president, watching him with cold eyes.

It was clearly meant as an insult. The proper form of address was Lord Cuelebre. The dragon almost smiled at such pettiness, but that might involve showing too many teeth. And if he did that, he did not think he would be able to resist a little snap at the air in front of her.

Instead, he deliberately dropped the vice president's honorific as he replied, "Mrs. Colton."

As he spoke, he took in an instinctive breath to mark the scent of his enemy . . . but caught no scent from either her or her husband.

No scent at all.

Instead, all he scented was a faint chemical stink.

Realization raged through his veins. Both the vice president and her husband had sprayed themselves with KO Odorless Odor Eliminator.

Deer hunters used the spray to mask their scent. So did Wyr criminals.

This time the dragon did show far too many teeth. He put his hand over Pia's as it rested in the crook of his arm, tightening his grip so hard he felt rather than heard her silent intake of breath.

He told the humans, "I look forward to having you for dinner tomorrow."

"We will be there." The vice president inclined her head in brusque acknowledgment.

Her manner clearly said they would be present because they had no other choice. As he spun Pia away from the other couple, she wiggled her fingers protestingly under the weight of his iron grip.

You look forward to "having them for dinner"? she asked silently, giving him a rebuking look. *Really, Dragos, you're not even trying.* She paused to search his expression. *What's wrong?*

He said, *Did you catch their scents?*

No, I— She paused thoughtfully and her eyebrows drew together. *No. Not at all.*

That's because they were masking them. He glanced down into her confused face and explained, *Human hunters mask their scents when they're hunting prey. And Wyr criminals mask their scents to avoid detection.*

Her confusion darkened into disquiet. *That's . . . why would they do that?*

That is a very good question, and one I would like to get answered. He switched mental gears and looked for Bayne. The sentinel stood several feet away, talking to Eva. Dragos said to him, *The vice president and her husband are masking their scents. I want to know why. And I want to know if there's anybody else present who is doing the same.*

Other than a quick flicker in his hard hazel eyes, the sentinel's expression never changed. Calmly, Bayne said, *I'm on it.*

Since the White House was protected by the Secret Service, protocol for the evening's function kept their individual security detail to two, one for each dignitary, which meant Bayne's investigative capabilities were limited.

Take Eva with you, said Dragos. *I'm staying with Pia.*

You got it, said Bayne. The sentinel touched Eva's arm

and the pair headed off, disappearing into the crowd.

Pia rubbed her thigh as she looked over the crowd. She said in a quiet voice meant for his ears alone, "Suddenly I don't feel like making nice or dancing with anybody."

Distracted from larger questions, he frowned as he looked down at her leg. "Why do you keep rubbing yourself like that?"

"You don't have to make it sound so dirty." She scowled back at him. "My leg itches. Do you have to take note of every little thing I do? I mean every tiny, little thing, Dragos."

"Yes," he said simply. "When I look at you, even when things are going to hell, somehow everything is all right."

"Ooh." Her grumpy gaze melted into warm affection. She stepped close to slip an arm around his waist and lean against him. A corner of her mouth tugged upward. "Even when you're about to put yourself in the doghouse over something, somehow you manage to say just the right thing and get yourself right out again."

He put an arm around her, hugging her briefly as he pressed his mouth to her forehead. "That's because you love me, and you hate having me in that doghouse anyway."

"True . . ." Then she focused behind him, and her expression transformed into such complete delight, he didn't have to turn around to know who was standing behind him. "Niniane!"

Pulling out from underneath his arm, Pia dashed

forward. He pivoted on one heel to watch her throw her arms around a petite, curvy Dark Fae woman. Niniane, or "Tricks" as she had been known when she had lived among the Wyr in New York, threw her arms around Pia with an excited squeal.

Before Dragos killed her uncle Urien, who had murdered her family and usurped the Dark Fae throne, Niniane had been a refugee at Wyr Court, living under Dragos's protection.

Back then, she had been prone to very high heels, sparkly sequins, marabou, and other kinds of feminine froufrou, but he saw that her tastes had sobered or matured somewhat since she had assumed the Dark Fae throne, at least in public.

Tonight, she wore richly embroidered Dark Fae traditional attire in subtle hues—a long, high-necked tunic over slim trousers. She had also let her black hair grow longer and wore it in an elegant chignon that bared long, pointed ears and emphasized her large, dark gray eyes. Nestled atop her sleek hairdo, she wore a thin circlet of sparkling sapphires, and she looked every inch a pocket-sized Dark Fae royal.

He was very pleased. Tricks did indeed look like she was thriving. For the first time since entering the White House, Dragos's smile turned real. He looked his attention from the embracing women to the enormous Wyr male who stood just behind them. Tiago also wore traditional Dark Fae attire, although his outfit was entirely black.

Bayne was right, Dragos thought, amused. All the

fresh air and prospect of political assassinations did seem to be doing Tiago a lot of good. He looked both relaxed and deadly, his dark skin burnished from good health and sunshine.

Once one of Dragos's seven sentinels, Tiago had mated with Niniane and went with her to live in the Dark Fae Other land of Adriyel.

When the Earth had been formed, time and space had buckled, creating Other lands that were connected to Earth and sometimes to each other by dimensional crossover passageways. They were magic-rich places where combustible technologies didn't work, and where time ran differently.

Sometimes the Other lands were immense, as Adriyel was, and they had several crossover passageways to other places. Sometimes the Other lands were mere pockets of space that led nowhere. Adriyel had significant time slippage from the rest of Earth, so that visits from Niniane and Tiago were rare.

As Tiago had been a Wyr sentinel and she had become the Dark Fae Queen, according to Dark Fae law, they could never marry, but neither had found that to be an impediment to their happiness. Tiago lived at her court as her chief of security.

In the face of Dragos's friends, the dragon's feral internal voice retreated into the shadows. Stepping forward, he clasped hands with Tiago. "You look good."

"You too," Tiago said, eyeing him with a glance of approval. He turned to survey the large, crowded ballroom. "Good job not killing anybody."

"That's what Pia said," Dragos told him. "Night's not over yet."

"I kinda love it more than I ever thought I could, especially since I have such bad memories from when my family was killed," Niniane was saying to Pia. "But I can't get over missing junk food. I have it shipped all the way to Adriyel. Reese's Peanut Butter Cups. Doritos. Skittles, and oh my gods, Hostess Ho Hos. And you just can't ship fresh-baked pepperoni pizza. I've been gorging on it ever since we arrived."

Dragos met Tiago's black gaze. "You ship Hostess Ho Hos to Adriyel?"

"They're very important," said Tiago impassively. "In fact, they have become quite the court fashion in Dark Fae circles. A single Ho Ho is now worth twenty Dark Fae doubloons. We're making a killing."

A bark of laughter burst out of Dragos, surprising him. Releasing Pia, Niniane turned to fling her arms around him. "Dragos! It's so, so, so good to see you! Come down here, I need to kiss you."

Obligingly, he bent and turned his head so that she could smack him on the cheek. She hugged him tightly again, and as he put his arms around her, he glanced at Pia, who was, after all, in the mating heat as well.

Her face had turned sour, and she sucked a tooth, but she didn't say anything. Still amused, he said in her head, *Okay there, lover?*

If it was anybody else but Niniane, I'm not sure I would be, she told him. *Thankfully, you're not very approachable to most people.*

At that, he cocked a sardonic eyebrow, but as she was right, he let it pass.

He caught sight of Bayne winding his way between clumps of people and told the others, "Excuse me."

Stepping away from the small group, he asked, *What did you find?*

Bayne shook his head. To a casual observer, he might still look relaxed, but Dragos knew him very well and caught the subtle tight compression to his mouth.

Bayne said, *I counted close to seventy people who are masking their scents, mostly congressmen and other officials and their spouses, along with a few interns. I cornered the White House press secretary, since Angela's always been on friendly terms with us. She said it started sometime early last week in a sub-faction of people who are against maintaining warmer relations with the Elder Races. They're calling it a Right to Privacy movement.*

Dragos rubbed the back of his neck. *Seventy fucking people, most of them government officials. That's a sub-faction?*

I know. Bayne met his gaze with a grim look. *Washington is pretty strongly divided on how to deal with the Elder Races right now. Rumor has it, Angela said, that the vice president started it. This is the president's last term in office, and she thinks Colton might be cultivating the issue to use it in her platform in a bid for election.*

Fucking hell. If Colton became president, the world for the Elder Races, and the Wyr in particular, would get very cold indeed.

Automatically, he scanned the crowd for Colton. As he was taller than most people, he was able to locate her easily, standing to one side of the large ballroom with a tall, lean man. They looked like they were having a tense conversation, perhaps even an argument.

He strained to hear what they might be saying, but even though he was very good at pinpointing something specific from some distance away, there were too many people, and the orchestra was too loud, for him to catch any of their conversation.

Who is that man standing with Colton? he asked Bayne.

The other man turned to follow his gaze. *I think that's her chief of staff, Aaron Davis.*

If he was Colton's chief of staff, then Davis would be coming to dinner tomorrow evening. Dragos's eyes narrowed. There might be something he could do to increase the tensions between the two. He would make a point of talking with Davis, to see if the other man's loyalties might be less than concretely fixed.

Anything else you need? Bayne asked.

No, not now, thanks. Circulate, and see if you can overhear anything useful.

Will do.

Bayne disappeared into the crowd again.

Deep in thought, Dragos joined Pia, Niniane and Tiago. Waitstaff threaded through the crowd, offering platters of hors d'oeuvres to people as they passed.

While Dragos responded to the conversation, and smiled when the others did, in the back of his mind, he began to lay plans.

If Colton announced a bid for the presidency, he was going to funnel money into every PAC he could find that operated against her candidacy.

Because he was always thinking of contingencies.

He played with budget numbers for a while, but ultimately set it aside as unsatisfactory and considered other options.

There was always assassination, of course. But assassination was tricky to pull off without having it backfire. If Colton announced a bid for the presidency and gained any traction—and even if she didn't—her death could potentially add fuel to her causes, which would eventually make everything worse.

No, assassination wasn't the most preferred course of action, at least not in this case. He could work to discredit her. Hire human spies to dig up dirt on her. That might have some merit, but it still wouldn't dispel the antipathy against the Elder Races and the Wyr that she had whipped up.

He needed to think of something else to address that particular problem. And in case that didn't work . . . what other contingency plans could he set into place?

Just then, Xavier del Torro, regent of the Nightkind demesne, and Tatiana, the Light Fae Queen, strolled up, and he set aside that train of thought with a mental note to pursue it later.

The evening passed in a grueling haze of forced pleasantries and hidden tensions.

And, occasionally, some not so hidden tensions.

The Light Fae Queen Tatiana apparently refused to talk to the Elven High Lord Ferion, not even in pleasantries, and she cut him dead when he approached. The gods only knew what that was about.

And at one point the head of the Demonkind assembly and the head of the witches demesne broke into a soft-voiced argument.

Jered and Isalynn's dislike for each other was well known. As they smilingly engaged in a quiet spat, Pia poked Dragos in the ribs and said in his head, *People are taking note of this. We'd better break them up.*

He almost rolled his eyes, but as he glanced around, he saw that Pia was right. Others were watching the two, some covertly but others with quite open, and not particularly friendly, interest.

Moving together with Pia, he took hold of Isalynn's arm and walked away with her while Pia distracted Jered.

Think of it. The dragon was practicing diplomacy.

He chuckled to himself, even as Isalynn hissed under her breath at him, "Let go of my arm, Dragos!"

"Not until you and Jered are far away from each other," he said. He switched to telepathy and said bluntly, *Pull your shit together, Isalynn, and smile at me like you mean it, because if you don't think we're on trial right now, you haven't been paying attention. And you're a lot more stupid than I thought.*

Damn it. You're insufferable at the best of times. I hate it when you're right. She took two short, angry breaths, then turned to show her teeth at him.

His cold gaze ran over her bold, attractive features. He didn't care that her dark gaze still snapped with anger and dislike. All her facial muscles had moved in a close approximation of a smile, and that was all anyone else would see.

He walked her over to a buffet table where they helped themselves to refreshments. As two congressmen approached, he left her to converse with them and circled back around to find Pia.

Pia did end up dancing twice, once with President Johnson, and a second time with Ferion, while both times Dragos held himself in a clench and managed not to bite anybody's head off.

Not even Johnson's relative age helped. Despite being a politician in his sixties, Johnson wasn't an old, ugly fucker. He was still a handsome, fit son of a bitch, and as he whirled Pia around the dance floor, she threw back her head and laughed more than once.

And watching her waltz with Ferion felt like someone just out of eyesight was raking talons down a blackboard. His hands tightened into fists as he imagined grinding the handsome Elf into the polished floor.

"Dragos, is that a flame I see coming out of your nostrils?" Niniane asked.

As he had been obsessing over Pia's dance, the little Queen had maneuvered to stand directly in front of him, her head tilted sideways as she squinted at him.

He sucked in a breath, swallowing down the fire, and growled, "I don't know what you're talking about."

"It was too. *That* was a tiny little flame." She pointed an accusing finger at his nose. "What are you trying to do, create a general panic and destroy everything everybody is trying to achieve here?"

"Of course not," he snapped. "I was holding myself in check, goddammit."

She considered him for a moment then said telepathically, *I actually believe you think you are. Tiago said you and Pia were in a mating phase.*

We are. Goddammit, of course Tiago with his sensitive sense of smell would pick up on that. Dragos might just buy some KO Odorless Odor Eliminator and join the Right to Privacy movement himself.

"Well, just so you know," Niniane said aloud, patting his arm, "I'm pretty sure I overheard Ferion and Pia setting up an assignation for tomorrow at noon, for somewhere called the Paradise Motel."

That snapped his gaze away from the dancing couple. He glowered at Niniane. "What the fuck are you talking about? Pia would never set up an assignation with Ferion."

"I know, right?" Niniane let out a peal of laughter. "Even smart men can be such dumbasses." When he glared at her, she sobered somewhat and told him, "Stuff that mating nonsense down deep somewhere before you do something stupid. I mean, Dragos . . . Pia and Ferion? Come on."

"You never used to talk to me that way when you lived in New York," he said, his eyes narrowed.

"I never used to do a lot of things before I became Queen," she said matter-of-factly. She gave him a small charming smile. "Besides, you like me, and I'm not telling you anything your brain isn't already telling your hormones. You'll deal with it."

"Dictatorial little shit," he muttered. "I don't see you dancing with anybody."

Her smile faded, and she looked sidelong at Tiago, who stood with his arms crossed, talking with Bayne.

"Yeah, well, I can call out irrational behavior, but I can't necessarily stop it, can I?" she muttered in reply.

That snagged his full attention. Turning away from watching Pia on the dance floor, he studied Niniane as he switched to telepathy. *Everything okay, pipsqueak?*

She gave him a quick smile. *Oh, everything's fine. Don't worry. Tiago and I just have a completely different relational dynamic than you and Pia. You and Pia are all out there—rings, public displays of affection, matrimony and a child, etc. But Tiago and I have to be more discreet about our relationship.*

He frowned and rubbed his jaw. *Is that a problem?*

She shook her head. *No, not as things stand currently. I'm pretty sure we're a well-known secret in Dark Fae society, but as long as we don't flaunt anything, they're accepting it. They're accepting him.*

That's good, he murmured.

It is, but there's always that slight tension, you know? He has to refrain from making any public statement of claiming me, and in return, I try to act with a little more sensitivity about things, like dancing with other males in public. We're balancing things just fine.

As he listened, his gaze fell on the vice president and her husband, dancing the waltz. He asked, *What if the balance shifts?*

Niniane's mental voice remained firm and strong. *We don't let it shift. Right now, we're both engaged, challenged and satisfied with our status quo. If we decide we want to do something else, or have a different definition of our lives and relationship, I'll abdicate and we'll go somewhere else.*

Go somewhere else.

They would have to, since, much as the Dark Fae had accepted Tiago for what he was, they would never accept a marriage between their Queen and a Wyr ex-sentinel. Curiously, he asked, *You could give up all that power, now that you have it?*

Absolutely, if it was the right thing for either Tiago or me—for us both. She gave him a quick smile. *And anyway, my point is, we're in a different place than you and Pia are. So even though you've got all those mating hormones running around in your dragony head, keep your sights fixed on why you and Pia broke up Jered and Isalynn before they came to blows. There's a lot at stake here.*

Point taken. He crossed his arms. *And, I might add—again—I haven't killed anybody yet. I should get credit for that.*

She patted him on the shoulder and switched to verbal speech. "Let's just keep it that way while we're all in D.C., 'kay?"

He shook his head grimly. "I'm doing my best, pipsqueak."

She snorted. "I'd say we're all probably doing our best to at least appear to get along. Which is pretty pathetic when you think about it. If you really have to eat somebody, at least please wait until Tiago and I leave for home again."

His mind switched gears. "You're not going to attend the Masque in New York?"

Annually, on the winter solstice, the Elder Races celebrated the Masque of the Gods. Dragos always threw a lavish party in the city for the event, and when Niniane lived with them, she used to love attending.

She sighed. "No, I'm afraid not. The solstice is still two months away, and we can't stay that long, not with the time slippage being what it is between Earth and Adriyel. We have things we need to attend to back at home."

"Understood." He crossed his arms. "Pia will be disappointed, but there isn't much that can be done about that."

She grinned up at him. "You'll just have to come visit us in Adriyel someday."

He raised an eyebrow. "That would be an interesting trip."

"I can just see it now," she declared, spreading out both hands. "Everybody would shit themselves to have the dragon come onto Dark Fae land. It would be *glorious*."

He barked out a laugh as the orchestra finally stopped playing that infernal waltz, and Ferion escorted his mate back to him.

She looked beautiful, as always, but underneath the bright vivacity of her makeup, she also looked tired. He put an arm around her. "We're done for the night."

"Are you sure?" she asked. Her gaze darted over the dance floor. "Nobody else has left yet, I don't think."

"Someone has always got to be the first," he replied. "Besides, it's almost eleven. We've put in a respectable enough showing."

"Okay." She leaned against him in relief.

They began the long, tedious process of saying their goodnights, until finally they were able to climb into the back of the limo and relax with big sighs. Eva and Bayne settled in the seats opposite them.

Bayne was the closest to the mini liquor cabinet. Dragos told him, "Pour me a double scotch, would you?"

"Sure." As Bayne handed the drink to him, he asked Pia, "You want anything?"

"Just water," she said. Her words disappeared into a wide yawn. "I guess for a fairly disastrous event, it didn't go too badly?"

Dragos snorted as he swallowed amber liquid and felt a pleasurable fire burn down his throat. "I guess you could say that."

Opening the cold water bottle that Bayne handed to her, she slid off her shoes and curled against Dragos's side. The soft, warm weight of her body resting against his felt soothing, and he let go of the tension that had tightened his muscles all evening.

She asked him telepathically, *What are we going to do if we can't smooth things over?*

I've been thinking of contingency plans all evening, he admitted. Finishing his drink, he held it out to Bayne in a silent request for another. He thought of the conversation he'd just had with Niniane. *We always said that if we needed to walk away from my position we would, but that wouldn't solve the problem for any of the other Wyr.*

No, she sighed. *In fact, it might make things worse for everybody else. If we walked away, I would want to take all of them with us.*

At that, an idea burgeoned in his head, and he went still as he thought it over.

It was sweeping and drastic, but it was also the first idea all evening that made his uneasiness subside.

If worst comes to worst, he promised, *we will take all the Wyr with us. At least, all the Wyr who want to come.*

Chapter Six

PIA LIFTED HER head to stare at him. He looked alert and focused, as he always did when his mind was racing.

She didn't know if she should be amused or maybe even a little frightened. She said uncertainly, *You do realize it's physically impossible to run away with the world's entire population of Wyr. Don't you? I mean, isn't it? Even if we could corral them all together. Oh lordy, that would be like trying to herd thousands of cats all at once.*

Chuckling, he kissed her. *Don't worry, worst is not going to come to worst.*

But if it did, she insisted.

If it did, I think we should take a leaf from the Dark Fae's example, he told her. *They never did invest entirely in integration into human society, which is why they have such a thriving culture in Adriyel.*

You mean leave New York? She felt her eyes widen. *Completely?*

He laced his fingers with hers. *You know our house in the Other land, the one where I like to experiment with what technologies can be brought over from Earth?*

She thought back. *You told me about it . . . last May, I*

think, but you haven't mentioned it since.

I've been too busy to tinker around with that project, he said. *But that land is massive. It's roughly the size of Greenland, only unlike Greenland, there's lots of arable farmland, lots of clean water, and clear, fresh skies, and almost no people. That's one of the reasons why I like it so much. More importantly, at least right now, the main access to the Other land is near our estate in upstate New York.* He met her gaze. *That land is mine, and it has limited entry points which makes it easily defensible, along with plenty of natural resources.*

She sat up straight as she turned the thought over in her mind. Yes, there was tremendous possibility, but there were huge obstacles as well.

She said slowly, *You're talking about transplanting a lot of people who don't know how to live without modern Earth technology. Many of them live in cities, and they buy their groceries along with everything else they need in stores.*

Well, I didn't say it would be easy, or that it should happen quickly, he replied. *Or even if it should happen at all. But if worst came to worst, and we couldn't find a way to continue living peacefully with humankind, we would have a place to go that would be safe and sustainable. I just need to hire a team of civil engineers and maybe some Dark Fae consultants to lay the groundwork, so that we're not caught completely vulnerable and unprepared.*

Oh yay, we get to build a whole new utopian society in our free time? She yawned again.

Potentially, he said, chuckling. *A whole new potential utopian society. If worst came to worst.*

I'll be honest, she confessed. *I'm too tired to really absorb an idea of this magnitude. I can't imagine the kind of infrastruc-*

ture you would need to lay down that would support thousands of people, let alone the training programs you would need to help them acclimate to such a different way of life.

That's okay. He hooked an arm around her and pulled her back against his side. *Because the worst isn't going to come to worst. Things will smooth over.*

She didn't believe him. Perhaps things might smooth over, but Dragos never relied on blind optimism as a viable course of action. She had no doubt that very trait was one of the reasons why he was still alive, and so successful.

Her heavy eyelids refused to remain open any longer and drifted shut. *You're still going to hire that cadre of civil engineers and consultants, though, aren't you?*

Hell, yes.

They might have only been together for eighteen months, but in some ways, they already knew each other so well. She smiled, and the smooth rhythm of the limo's engine lulled her to sleep.

When she woke up again, they had arrived back at the Wyr residence and he was carrying her up the magnificent staircase. He had slipped her high heeled shoes off, and they rested on her stomach.

"Shades of Rhett Butler," she muttered, putting her hand on the shoes to make sure they didn't slip off and fall to the floor.

"What's that?" He bent his head toward her. "I'm sorry I woke you."

"*Mmph.* Don't be sorry." She yawned again. "I have to get ready for bed anyway."

He rested his cheek against the top of her head. "I was going to zip you out of your dress."

Her tired body pulsed at the idea, but overpowering as the mating instinct could be when it held her in its grip, instead of perking up, she felt rather ill. Scratching her thigh, all she could look forward to was shedding the Dior so she could spread some lotion over her itchy skin.

"Much as I would love to," she mumbled, "I'm too exhausted tonight."

"I wasn't suggesting we do anything." He used her feet to push open the bedroom door and carried her inside. "We both need a good night's sleep to face tomorrow and the rest of this week."

He set her gently on the end of the bed, and she braced her body upright with both hands planted on the mattress. "We have all those horrible people coming over here for dinner. Actually, I like several of them individually. It's just that so many of them don't like each other, and when they all get together, all these squabbles break out." She rubbed her forehead as she thought of the Coltons. "Only some of them are just plain horrible."

"Don't think about that right now." He shed his jacket and pulled off his tie with a sigh. "Think about crawling between nice, cool sheets and turning off the light."

As she was thinking of the Coltons anyway, her mind went to what had happened earlier, and she started to snicker.

"What?" He glanced at her curiously as he stripped off his shirt.

She deepened her voice to mimic him. *"I look forward to having you for dinner tomorrow."*

A wicked grin lit his hard face. "The look on their faces was my one pleasure of the evening."

While he strolled into the bathroom to brush his teeth, she went to sit at the vanity to smooth cleansing cream over her face. As she wiped off the cream and makeup with tissues, her true complexion appeared. She looked dead-fish white, with blotchy areas where she had been rubbing her skin and dark circles under her eyes.

She made a face at herself in the mirror. When Dragos got tired, he just looked more rugged and dangerously sexy, with a piratical hint of dark beard shadowing his lean cheeks. When she was exhausted, she looked like something a cat might throw up.

He left the bathroom, totally nude, and climbed into bed, and it was her turn to use the bathroom. She forced herself upright and went to brush her teeth as well, and splash the last of the cream off her face. Her skin was still blotchy from where she had rubbed it with tissues. She frowned at her reflection and shimmied out of her dress.

Then she reached for her body lotion and propped her foot on the rim of the bathtub to rub lotion on her irritated skin.

A large bright, angry red patch covered the expanse of her thigh. Freezing, she stared at her leg. Then she looked over her shoulder again at the reflection of her still blotchy face.

"Oh, God," she sighed. This was the last thing she

needed.

She hadn't said it very loudly, but her mate had ears sharper than any other creature she had ever personally met. Dragos said from the bedroom, "What is it?"

"I'm all blotchy," she complained.

He appeared in the doorway, frowning as he took in her appearance. "Did you eat any of the hors d'oeuvres?"

"Yes, but I made sure to ask if they were vegan first. I always do."

His frown deepened as he touched her leg with one forefinger. He motioned for the bottle, and when she handed it to him, he began to spread body lotion gently over her leg. "Recipes can be sneaky. Maybe the servers made a mistake, and something had a trace of meat, fish or dairy in it. Do you feel nauseated at all?"

She was vegan, not only by choice, but by nature too. Her digestive system simply didn't recognize any meat, fish, or dairy products as food.

"No, but I'm still wearing the diamond necklace." She made a face at him. "I don't want to be blotchy this week, not while the world's going to hell in a handbasket."

He studied her with narrowed eyes. "Take the necklace off."

Sighing, she complied. As soon as the pendant left contact with her skin, her stomach heaved. Tossing it with a clatter onto the nearby counter, she lunged for the toilet.

While she struggled to rid herself of everything in her stomach, strong hands came down on her, one cupping her forehead and the other bracing her back. Feeling too sick to indulge in self-consciousness, after she finished vomiting, she leaned her trembling body against his large, steadier frame.

"That was utterly vile," she muttered.

He stroked the damp hair off her face. "It's better to throw up than have it take the long way through your system. Hopefully after a good night's sleep, you'll feel better by morning."

"True."

After he helped her to her feet, she brushed her teeth again and followed him to bed. He opened his arms to her, and she crawled over to curl around his long, stretched out frame. Comfort sank deep. Nuzzling the bare, warm skin of his shoulder, she closed her eyes.

Just before she fell asleep, the tired fog lifted from her mind and she remembered.

She had been nauseated well before eating the hors d'oeuvres that evening, and her skin had begun to feel irritated too.

Time to make an appointment to see Dr. Medina when they got back home.

Then darkness called, and she was unable to resist its inexorable pull.

WHEN AWARENESS DAWNED next, she discovered that she had curled on her side, and Dragos lay spooning her from behind. The room lay in deep shadow, although a sliver of light at the edge of the curtain indicated it was close to dawn.

His warm mouth traveled across the nape of her neck, while he stroked her torso from breast to hip. His large, hot erection pressed against her buttocks.

"Good morning, lover," he whispered in her ear. "How are you feeling—any better?"

"*Mmm*," she murmured, luxuriating in a long, all-over body stretch that might also have made her brush all along the length of his body as well. She adored the feeling of his body next to hers, dark bronze skin covering sleek, iron hard muscles and sprinkled with black, silken hair. It was beyond a doubt the very best way to wake up in the mornings. Rolling onto her back, she rubbed her face against his chest. "Still tired, but okay."

He cupped her breast and pressed a gentle kiss against the jut of her nipple. "Okay enough for this?"

She took stock. Her muscles ached and her thigh still itched, but none of it could dispel a growing sense of hunger for him. "I want to," she admitted. "But I don't feel very rambunctious."

"We'll go slow and easy this time," he promised. "I can do all the work. You can lie back and count your *pows*."

Delighted, she snickered as she tilted her face up for his kiss. "You offer a bargain so good I can't resist."

He cupped the back of her head, supporting her neck as he slanted his mouth over hers and kissed her gently, deeply. A sense of golden well-being suffused her, physical pleasure mingling with the emotional.

He was so good, so good. He was more fierce and

demanding than anyone else she had ever known, but he was also the tenderest of lovers too, and he handled her as if she were a treasure beyond compare.

It was impossible to maintain worry when she was in his arms, impossible to hold on to anything negative or isolating. When they were together, they were all in, utterly immersed in each other, invested completely in this intangible, essential thing they had developed between them. Nothing else existed.

Trailing light kisses along her body, he nipped at her breasts gently and suckled at the stiff, sensitive peaks of her nipples. While he caressed and licked at her, she quested down his body with one hand, running her fingers through the silken tract of hair low on his tight, flat abdomen until she located his erection.

Closing her fingers around his cock, she massaged the long, thick length. His skin felt like silk stretched over iron. Using the ball of her thumb, she rubbed circles along the broad tip of his penis.

In response, he exhaled hard and flexed his hips so that he pushed against the palm of her hand, while his mouth traveled up the line of her neck to caress her lips again.

He wasn't a man filled with soft words or poetry, and it was rare for him to say that he loved her. But he told her in so many different ways, the lack of soft words and poetry never mattered, not in the slightest.

He told her through the touch of his lips, and the depth of emotion expressed in every caress of those callused, powerful hands. He told her in the amount of attention he paid to every detail of her life, and the way his hard face would light up whenever she entered a room.

He told her every time he put his arm around her, or complained at her absence. This, from a male who did not tolerate the presence of others very well in general.

In a thousand different ways, he made her feel cherished and valued, and this bout of lovemaking was no different. He was as good as his word, and even though she could feel his rising heat and hunger, running like lava underneath his skin and hardening his big, tough frame, he never once broke out of the gentle pace he set for himself.

Using just his fingers, he stroked her to climax, and only when she had eased out of the shaking pulse of completion did he come between her legs to settle his hips against hers and push into her entrance easily, carefully.

A hot wave of emotion washed through her as she felt his cock entering her. Both physical and emotional pleasure lit her up entirely. She wound her arms and legs around him, cradling him with her whole body, trying to tell him without words just how important he was to her too.

At this one place, their conversation was unchanging.

Here I am, her cradling body said to him. I'll be your home.

Looking deep into her eyes, he began to move. Here I am, his body said to her. I'll cover you and keep you safe.

At this one place, his normal possessive nature shifted. At any other time, he told her in a dozen ways, you are mine.

But here, in this one place, he told her, I'm yours.

His own climax took him over, and he gave it to her. She watched him without blinking, without hardly breathing, stroking his face as he gave her everything he had.

After staying with her for long moments, he eased away, reached for the tissues on the bedside table, and helped her to clean off her inner thighs. Then he pulled her with him, so that they rested with their legs entwined. Utterly drained and satisfied in the best way possible, she buried her face against his chest and fell deeply asleep again.

When she woke next, she was alone in the bed. Rolling over, she took stock of her immediate surroundings. While the room still remained in deep shadow, a bright yellow band of sunlight along the edges of the curtains told her the day had advanced significantly.

Dragos wasn't anywhere in the room. The open door to the bathroom revealed that it was empty and quiet. He had left her to sleep in.

She *tsked* softly, partly in exasperation but mostly in contentment. There was so much to do that day—so much—but she couldn't deny that it had felt really good to get her sleep out.

As she rolled to her side of the bed, she saw a piece of paper resting on the bedside table. Picking it up, she saw that it was covered with Dragos's bold scrawl.

No need to come with me this afternoon. Try to relax today. The staff can take care of everything for tonight. – D

Try to relax, when the president, the vice president, the speaker of the House, both the majority and minority leaders of the Senate, and all the demesne leaders, along with their spouses and personal security retinues were coming to the Wyr residence for dinner?

"I love you," she told the note. "But sometimes you are a foolish, foolish man. Although undeniably a very handsome, sexy one."

Kissing the paper, she set it aside, called down to the kitchen to request a pot of coffee and a bowl of fresh fruit and then she got out of bed.

As soon as she stood upright, nausea punched her, hard and wicked, and more powerful than ever. She bolted to the bathroom, and her body twisted into wretched spasms.

Finally, she was able to sit back on the floor and take in a deep breath. Instinctively, she scanned her body again. Still no baby.

She didn't have time to mourn the lack of a tiny life spark within her. Damn it. Damnity damn damn it. Her leg itched furiously, and as she scratched it, the itching grew even worse. She looked down at herself.

Her thigh was redder than ever, a dark, angry color, and covered in bumps.

A knock sounded at the door. Pia rolled to her feet. Swirling nausea gripped her by the throat. She grabbed for the diamond pendant, slung it on, and the nausea subsided. She called out, "Who is it?"

"Eva. I've got your breakfast tray."

Her bathrobe hung on a hook on the back of the bathroom door. She snatched it and put it on. "Come in."

The door opened, and Eva carried the tray inside. As the other woman set it on the bedside table, Pia strode up to her and yanked one flap of the robe aside to bare her thigh. "What is this?" she demanded. "Do you know?"

Eva turned to look at her leg, and her eyebrows rose. After a moment's thought, she replied, "Looks likes hives to me."

"Hives?" Pia was trying to avoid scratching at it, but the itching was driving her crazy. "Isn't that what happens when you're allergic to something?"

"Yeah. What'd you do, eat something you shouldn't have?"

"No." She frowned. She had also never before had such an extreme reaction to eating something she shouldn't. "At least I don't think so."

"Well, if you're allergic to something, you might react within a couple of hours, but it can take up to seventy-two hours for food poisoning to set in, so you could be reacting to something you ate as long as three days ago," Eva said. "It could take you a couple of days to get over it."

Pia tried to think back, but she had no idea what she had eaten three days ago. She hadn't been paying attention . . . although she was pretty sure she had eaten everything from home that day, so the food should have been safe.

She growled in frustration and dashed back to the bathroom to look at her reflection. Her skin was still pale and blotchy. She threw up her hands. Great, just bloody great.

"Maybe you should see a doctor?" Eva had followed her to the bathroom and was watching her with a troubled expression.

"See a Wyr doctor in D.C.?" Snorting, she turned away from the offending mirror. "Good luck finding one. Humans take over-the-counter medication for allergies. It's called antihistamines. Have you heard of it before?"

Eva rubbed her face. "Yeah."

Her gaze met Eva's. "I'll put in a call to Dr. Medina, but in the meantime, get me some antihistamines. I don't care what brand. I'm going to make it through this day if it kills me."

But first, she was going to take a shower to see if that would calm down the infernal itching, at least until Eva could get back with the medication. Eva took off, while she showered, smothered her leg in lotion and dressed in jeans and a light silk sweater.

Thank the gods, Dragos had taken off some time ago to attend the day's functions without her. She drank a quick cup of coffee, ate a few bites of fruit, and called the doctor's office.

Dr. Medina was busy dealing with an emergency, the

office manager told her, but she would be sure to return Pia's call as soon as she could. Pia hung up, went to the vanity and smoothed another ten pounds of makeup on her face to hide her blotchy complexion, until she looked more or less normal.

Then Eva returned with several different packages of antihistamines. Together, they scanned the dosage directions.

"Don't operate any heavy machinery, may cause drowsiness. . . ." Eva read aloud.

Pia popped a dose out of foil wrap and swallowed them. "Or in other words, keep the coffee coming."

"You sure you feel up to this?" Eva pursed her lips in concern.

"I am totally up for this," Pia said grimly. "Let's go."

With that, she plunged into the day's preparations. It seemed that everyone had saved up at least a dozen questions to ask her. There was a mistake on the order of fresh flowers. Would the substitutes do? What about the seating arrangements for dinner?

Thankfully, her leg stopped itching after about a half an hour or so. When the doctor returned her call, a couple of hours later, she was so busy she let the phone call roll to voice mail. She could call Dr. Medina back in the morning.

The afternoon sped by too fast. Dragos arrived back at the residence in a foul mood. He was standing in the middle of the foyer watching staff scurry past, his hands on his hips, when Pia found him.

"How did your day go?" she asked.

"I hate people."

He sounded grumpy, but no more than usual when he had to deal with a lot of people. She held her face up to him. He took his time kissing her and did such a thorough job, she was flushed and laughing when he finally lifted his head again. "How are things going here?"

She looked around. "You might not be able to tell by looking, but it's a controlled kind of panic. It's just as well I didn't go with you today—there was too much to do here, but I think I can let go and get ready for the evening now. Come upstairs with me?"

"I will in a minute. I'm going to get a scotch, and I want to talk to Bayne first."

"Okay." She left him to jog up the stairs to their suite.

Last night, the outfit she wore was classic chic. Tonight, should she go romantic and wear the midnight blue dress? Or perhaps sophisticated with the silk taupe pantsuit?

Upstairs, the bedroom had been cleaned and straightened, and the packages of antihistamines had been stacked on the bedside table. Seeing them reminded her.

She kicked off her jeans to inspect her thigh. It hadn't itched for several hours, but the patch of skin was still red and angry looking. So, the hives had gone down some, but the irritation wasn't gone. She was masking a symptom, not eradicating the problem.

Sighing, she grabbed at the open package. After double-checking the instructions, she swallowed another dose.

There was no way she was going to try to take off the pendant at this point. Later tonight, she could take it off and see how she was really doing then.

Because nothing short of a full-scale natural disaster was going to keep her from getting through the dinner party this evening.

Chapter Seven

DOWNSTAIRS, DRAGOS RAN over security plans for the evening with Bayne. Every Wyr would be on duty that night to make sure the perimeter of the property was guarded tightly. All the nearby streets were cordoned off for three blocks in every direction, and guards were mounted on the tops of nearby buildings.

Inside, while the house was too old to have a modern-day security system running through the walls, Bayne had installed tiny hidden wireless cameras in every room, which were monitored in the security room in the basement, behind the wine cellar. The house's Wi-Fi network was a closed system, and it was backed up with an electric generator and a second server. They were as secure as modern technology could make them.

None of it calmed the dragon's uneasiness at staying in an unfriendly city. All the security in the world wouldn't protect the building from a long-range missile strike.

That was an extreme, highly unlikely scenario, but extreme shit happened. While he knew that the other demesnes, along with the different human police agencies, would also be on high alert throughout the city, he didn't like to trust his safety or that of his mate to other people's efforts.

Compulsively, he went below to make sure the openings to every tunnel had not been accidentally blocked off by all the trunks, boxes and furniture accrued over the last hundred and twenty years.

Yes, he was paranoid, but he had also been hunted before, several times throughout the ages. Being paranoid and untrusting had kept him alive, and he was vitally interested in maintaining that status quo.

Finally, he went upstairs to find the bedroom in chaos.

Pia had thrown different outfits along with matching jewelry sets on the bed. Small cardboard boxes littered one of the tables. As he raised his eyebrows and looked around, he found her crouched in front of the closet. She was wearing her dressing gown, her hair was rolled up in the hot curlers again, and she was busy pulling out shoes.

All her shoes. As far as he could tell, when she stood up, she carried in her arms every pair that she had brought on the trip.

As she caught sight of him, she muttered, "I'm so behind. I thought I was going to wear either the midnight blue dress or the silk pantsuit, but now neither one seems right, and I can't make up my mind!"

She threw her armful of shoes on the floor beside the bed.

He walked up behind her and put his arms around her. Her body vibrated with tension. He tightened his grip on her. The hot curlers hampered his desire to put his mouth in her hair, so instead, he put his mouth to the hollow where her neck met her shoulder.

"You're wound a little tight there, lover," he murmured.

"Yeah, sorry. I've downed a bucket of coffee today." She leaned back against him. "All of them are going to be here, Dragos—all of them under our roof."

"I know." He pressed a kiss against her warm skin.

"Has that ever happened before?"

"No, it hasn't. We've had a majority of leaders at functions and meetings before, but not every head of state in the continental U.S. at once."

She gave a reluctant chuckle. "You could have told me a reassuring lie. I'm sorry I'm being such a flake. I was fine until about fifteen minutes ago, and then I dissolved into this big ball of nerves."

"You're going to be amazing tonight," he told her. Pia didn't have a fancy political science degree, but she had good instincts about people, so he asked curiously, "I meant to ask you earlier but forgot—what did you think of Johnson when you danced together?"

The tension in her body eased somewhat. "You know, I liked him. Of course we didn't talk about anything very important, and I know he's known for being charming, but still he seems to have a core of real decency. He didn't try to disguise his scent, and just the fact that he asked me to dance says that he has a moderate stance to us—not only the Wyr, but also the Elder Races in general, I think."

He nodded slightly, while still maintaining contact on

her skin with his mouth. "That's been my impression too. I think he's genuinely concerned about the outbreaks of violence that have occurred over the last two years, and he wants to work together to minimize the risk of further violence in the future. And another positive—neither he, nor his wife, are participating in the Right to Privacy movement."

"It sounds like you had a productive day today," she said, reaching back to stroke his cheek.

"We did, I think." He lifted his head to consider the outfits strewn over the bed. "Wear the midnight blue dress. The blue almost matches your eyes, and I like how you look in it."

She let out a big sigh that sounded relieved. "I should let you pick out all my outfits this week. It'll save me a lot of time."

He grinned. "As long as I get to pick out your lingerie too, you're on."

"Okay, but you'd better hurry," she muttered. "I mean it. I'm going to be downstairs in twenty minutes. Other people can afford to be late, but not the hosts."

Obligingly, he turned to the dresser that held her intimate apparel. As he did so, his gaze fell on the small boxes on the nearby table. He asked, "By the way, what are these boxes?"

She threw a glower at the boxes as she rushed to the vanity table to pull out the hot curlers. "They're antihistamines for my rash."

"So it hasn't disappeared yet?"

"No," she sighed. "Maybe it will be gone by tomorrow."

He pulled out a dark blue bra and matching panties, relishing the feel of the silken material. Later, he would take these off her after she stepped out of that shimmery dress. At the thought, his cock stood at attention, but she was right. He didn't have time to indulge the urge.

Later, he promised himself.

Turning around to offer the lingerie to her, he asked, "Have the antihistamines helped any?"

"Sort of. The itching is a little better, at least so that I can ignore it when I'm busy, but the rash hasn't gone. I called Dr. Medina, but she was in an emergency, so if the rash isn't gone by morning, I'll call her again." She snatched the lingerie from him, pulled off her dressing gown and dressed swiftly.

He had to look away from the luscious sight of her tucking her full, pale breasts into that sexy bra. Focusing on her leg instead, he frowned at how much skin the dark red rash covered. "Call her anyway, even if the rash calms down. I want to know what she has to say."

"Okay." She shimmied into the dress and put her back to him. "Zip me up?"

"With pleasure." He helped her with the zipper and placed a final kiss at the back of her neck. Then he changed into a clean suit, a darker one more suitable for the evening, and as they left the bedroom, the dragon surfaced again in his mind.

He had once been much more feral, but age had taught him how to appreciate the more delicate aspects of warfare conducted over a well-cooked meal.

Because he had no doubt of it—while some of his guests tonight would be more moderate and open-minded, other guests were definitely waging war against him.

Tonight was his best chance to study them in order to discover the best way to defeat them.

If that included destroying them in the process, well then, so be it.

✧ ✧ ✧

AS THE FIRST of the guests arrived in a flurry of greetings, for the dozenth time that day, Pia did another mental head count of everybody attending.

The humans attending were the president, vice president, their respective chiefs of staff, the Senate majority and minority leaders, and the speaker of the House, along with all their spouses or plus ones.

On the Elder Races side—and even though Isalynn LeFevre was human, as head of the witches demesne, she counted personally and politically as one of the Elder Races—all seven of the demesne leaders were present, along with their spouses or plus ones.

Neither the Elder tribunal nor any of the members of the Supreme Court were involved in this week's talks, just those involved in active governance.

So there were fourteen and fourteen. Then there was the security staff, but they didn't count in terms of making sure glasses were refilled and seating arrangements at the dinner table.

Big and stately though the mansion was, it didn't have the sheer space or capacity to hold the high numbers that the White House could, and after some discussion and negotiation, most of everybody's security details awaited them outside, while each couple was allowed one person indoors, which made thirteen extra bodies to account for as a total head count.

Dragos and Pia's security didn't factor into that number, for their security staff was also the waitstaff. They threaded through the guests, offering hors d'oeuvres, wine and mixed drinks with polite smiles and watchful, smiling eyes. No expense had been spared for this evening. Five hundred dollar bottles of wine flowed like water, and only the highest quality liquors were offered to those who chose to partake.

When someone—Pia didn't catch who—suggested they open the large French-style doors and enjoy the unseasonably warm evening outside, Dragos moved to open the doors up and people spilled out onto the wide terrace.

In anticipation of doing just that, earlier that afternoon, when they were sure the weather was going to hold, Pia had worked with the staff to set out tables covered with white cloths, bouquets of fresh flowers and candles. After the doors had been opened, Bayne walked from table to table, lighting candles, until the terrace and the half-acre of manicured gardens were lit with sparks of soft, golden light.

Sipping with moderation at a glass of French Bordeaux, Pia circulated too, joining conversations briefly with small clusters of people before moving on to the next, while her gaze kept roaming constantly to make sure everyone was getting his or her needs met.

Aside from polite smiles and the most basic greeting, she avoided the vice president and her husband altogether—she wouldn't be able to change the Coltons' minds about anything, and she felt no need to engage with them. Thankfully they were Dragos's problem, not hers, and while she was happy to work to support him in what he did, she wouldn't change places with him for the world.

After the first forty-five minutes, the tight knot between her shoulder blades started to ease. Relations between humankind and the Elder Races might not be improved after this week, but that wouldn't be because of any fault in this evening.

At least she devoutly hoped not. Because, as Dragos would say, night's not over yet.

Then Gennita, the head chef, appeared in the open French doors and said discreetly in Pia's head, *My lady? When would you like for us to serve?*

How about in fifteen minutes? she replied.

Very good. I'll put the soufflés in the oven now, and we'll be ready. Gennita slipped away.

Pia could hear a high, constant buzzing in her ears, which was incredibly annoying. She didn't know if it was from nerves or the antihistamines, but she had no time for either. Abruptly, she set her glass of wine aside on one of the small tables, turned and came face-to-face with Tatiana, the immaculate, chic and—at least to her—

rather frightening Light Fae Queen.

"I've always envied Dragos this property," Tatiana told Pia, as she sipped a glass of sparkling wine. "Dragos certainly made all the right decisions at the right time when he bought the land and hired the architect. Now, of course, the place would sell for tens of millions of dollars—not that he's in the market to sell it, of course. But if he ever is, do get in touch with me, won't you?"

The Light Fae Queen wore a backless dress the deep, rich color of claret. It emphasized her golden skin, hourglass figure, and the dark curling hair she had pinned high at the back of her head. Secretive shadows seemed to flicker in her lovely, famous eyes, or perhaps that was just the effect of the night breeze on the nearby candles.

There were actually only twelve attendees on the Elder Races side, as Tatiana's only companion that evening was the captain of her guard, Shane Mac Carthaigh. Or was he her plus one? He was certainly doing double duty that evening, but Pia wasn't sure how to categorize him socially.

The Light Fae Queen showed not a single hint of discomfort at the evening's gathering, either in her beautiful, composed face or in her scent, while Pia felt circles of damp sweat soaking in her dress under her arms.

Envying the other woman her poise, she told Tatiana, "We'll be sure to let you know, if he ever decides to sell. I think I've stuck my head in every room and closet now, at least once, and everything is this beautiful. The attention to detail is everywhere."

"I can imagine." Tatiana studied her. "You interest me, young woman. You have a very interesting story that you've chosen not to share with the world. Dragos must see something very special about an herbivore of unknown nature. I always thought if he were to mate, it would be with one of the long-lived predators."

Pia slid a wary sidelong glance at the other woman. Instead of indulging in polite pleasantries, the Light Fae Queen had zeroed in on one of the Cuelebres' most touchy subjects.

Instead of getting more nervous, however, Pia suddenly relaxed. Both she and Dragos had been dodging questions like that from theWyr for the last eighteen months, and while she used to fumble much more in the beginning, by necessity she'd had to learn to grow a thick skin about the topic.

She gave Tatiana a smile. "You know, I would have thought that too, but it's funny how things work out. Speaking of which, I've been meaning to ask you—is Captain Shane your plus one, or your bodyguard for the evening?"

"Does he have to be one or the other?" Tatiana's smiling gaze met hers over the rim of her champagne flute.

"In reality, of course not," Pia told her. "But for dinner plans, yes, I'm afraid he does. Will he be joining us at the table?"

"He would be welcome to, as far as I'm concerned, but I think he would prefer to stand guard."

She inclined her head in thanks. "That's what I needed to know. If you'll excuse me, I need to go make a slight adjustment to the table."

"Of course," Tatiana replied. "You're on duty too, this evening. Everything is lovely, by the way. I do hope we get a chance to chat further sometime this week."

"That's very kind of you," Pia told her. As she left the other woman on the terrace, she muttered soundlessly to herself, *Not if I have anything to say about it, we won't.*

The Light Fae Queen was too curious about things that didn't concern her, and she didn't appear to have any compunction about pursuing them. Pia had fended her off for now, but she didn't have any doubt that Tatiana would circle back around to the subject if it suited her to do so.

Irritably, Pia went in search of someone to flag down to tell them about the place setting, but either the waitstaff were outside with most of the guests, or the kitchen staff were racing madly about, putting final preparations on the salmon soufflés that would be served as the first course.

Or, in Pia's case, a vegan spinach soufflé. While Pia had no idea how to cook one, apparently there was such a thing.

After a few moments, she gave up. It would be quicker and easier if she just took care of things herself.

In any case, she could use a few minutes alone. She felt tired, strung out from all the coffee she had drunk earlier, and the buzzing in her ears was driving her crazy.

She stepped into the dining room and paused to admire the long table, decorated with runners of fresh white roses, and beautifully set with antique bone china, polished silver and cut crystal Italian glasses. Long white candles would be lit just before guests came in.

After dithering over which place setting to pull, she gently gathered up a setting in the middle of the table on the side nearest the entrance to the kitchen. Everything—crystal, china so thin she could see light through it and the silver—was original to the building of the house, kept in perfect condition, fragile and irreplaceable, so she held the pieces with nervous care.

Instead of spreading the other place settings out and disrupting the balance of the table, maybe they could find something decorative to set in the empty spot. There might be more of the white roses in the kitchen, or maybe a candle.

Hell, at this point, she didn't care. They would throw something in the space.

Standing there, with her hands filled with bone china, silverware and crystal, her impetus ran out, while her thinking grew confused and jumbled.

The . . . there was a cabinet in the butler's pantry. . . .

No, that butler's pantry was in their home in upstate New York. Not in this house.

She blinked down at the pretty, foreign pieces in her hands. She couldn't remember where anything went.

"This doesn't matter," she muttered grimly, as the wheels in her head ground to a halt and refused to move. "Solve it and move on."

Someone in the kitchen would know what to do with

the place setting. They could take care of it after they dealt with the soufflés. For now, she could just shove it in a closet somewhere.

There weren't any closets in the dining room, so she hurried out into the hall. There was a rear closet in the hall, in an area near the kitchen, that held a built-in, hidden secretary desk where historically the housekeeper had kept household records. At least her tired brain remembered that much. It would do for now.

As she came within a few feet of the closet door, she smelled blood.

Fresh blood.

Which made no sense. There were doors opening and shutting all over the house, and in any case the meat dish wasn't going to be served until the third course. Why would the scent of blood linger in this quiet nook of the hallway?

Propping the place setting carefully under her arm, she opened the closet door, and flicked on the light as she stepped inside.

Oh, well, there was the fresh blood. Quite a lot of it, spilled in a massive puddle on the floor.

It came from the lacerated throat of Mr. Colton, the vice president's husband, who sat against the farthest wall in an ungainly sprawl, his head leaning far to one side. His white shirt was soaked in the blood that had pooled on the floor.

She blinked down at the wet, sticky pool of blood she stood in.

Then she set the place setting gently, oh so gently on

the narrow secretary desk.

Mr. Colton still looked surprised. She wasn't sure her legs were going to support her for much longer. The buzzing in her ears grew louder.

Dragos, she said telepathically.

Yes? Where are you? His mental voice sounded far away. *I thought you were outside with us.*

I was, she said. *But now . . .*

How exactly does one break the news to her husband that she's standing in a closet with the dead body of one of their dinner guests?

Something's come up, she told him. *You'd better come inside.*

Chapter Eight

I'M IN THE *middle of something.* He sounded impatient. *Is the house on fire?*

She considered that. Metaphorically, in a way, it was, with one of those sneaky house fires that smoldered in a tucked away corner but would blow their lives apart in, say, the next half hour or so.

The world wobbled, and she grabbed at the back of the chair that was tucked tight against the desk. She could feel Mr. Colton's blood beginning to soak into her shoes.

She didn't want to contaminate the scene any more than she already had. Swallowing hard, she eased one foot out of a shoe and stepped backward, out of the closet. As soon as she felt balanced enough on her bare foot, she stepped out of the other shoe.

Pia?

Yes, she told him. *The house is actually on fire. In a manner of speaking.*

Even as she said it, she heard voices as people approached.

" . . . you are asking the wrong person to explain human behavior, Jered," Niniane said. "Out of all of us,

Pia's the best to ask—she's the one who lived as a human for so many years. I'm sure I saw her come this way a few minutes ago . . ."

Oh gods. Conflicting impulses careened inside.

What should she do?

Jump in the closet and hide until they passed? No!

Where are you? Dragos asked. His voice had changed. No longer impatient, he sounded sharp and totally engaged.

Just as Niniane, Jered and Tiago rounded the corner, she slammed the closet door and rushed toward them.

"Hi, sweetie," Niniane said. Her gaze fell to Pia's feet, and her eyebrows went up. "Where are your shoes?"

With the dead man in the closet.

"I h-had an accident." Pia pressed shaking hands against her stomach.

Jered, a tall, blond male Djinn with diamondlike eyes, demanded, "Can you explain why we are all here to talk when some of those humans won't engage in conversation?"

PIA, Dragos thundered in her head, making her jump.

She snapped at him shakily, *Don't yell at me like that!*

Tiago said suddenly, "I smell blood."

Well, of course he did. He had, if anything, a more refined sense of smell for such things than Pia did.

"Blood?!" Niniane exclaimed.

It was pointless to try to assert control over something so outrageous, but Pia tried anyway. She said, "Yes, well, there is a problem. I mean, I found a p-problem. I don't suppose I could convince any of you to go back outside and keep everyone busy while Dragos and I deal with it?"

Niniane grabbed her by the arms. "Are you hurt?"

"It's not her blood," Tiago said.

Pia had tried to position herself in the middle of the hallway to act as a barrier, but he shouldered past her. So much for her attempt to gain a little time.

Closing her eyes, she listened as the closet door opened.

After a moment, Tiago said, "It's his blood."

"What on earth are you talking about?" Niniane's grip fell from Pia's arms.

She turned to watch as Niniane and Jered swept past her. Tiago took a step to one side, and all three of them stared into the closet.

Dragos rounded the corner, wearing a fierce frown. "Why didn't you answer me?" he demanded, dropping a hand onto her shoulder. "Where's the damn fire that won't wait?"

Wordlessly, she pointed back down the hall to where the other three stood. As Dragos looked behind her, Niniane pointed into the closet. After a moment, both Tiago and Jered pointed too.

Pia said between her teeth, "I am really going to love living in our version of Greenland. I bet it's peaceful there. The murder rate can't be anything like D.C.'s."

Dragos's hand tightened on her before it fell away. He strode forward to join the others and looked in the closet.

Niniane said to Tiago, "Once upon a time, I would have been so much more shaken than I am right now. I thought we were going to get a break from this kind of shit on this trip."

"You know, as your chief of security, I have to advise you that we leave right now," Tiago told her.

"We can't leave!" Niniane exclaimed. "That would make us look like we have something to hide."

"I don't give a damn what it looks like, your argumentativeness." Tiago crossed his arms. "Someone has been killed. It's a safety recommendation."

"Fine." She rolled her eyes. "Duly noted."

Dragos's gaze met Pia's. His expression looked calm but she knew from his incandescent, molten gaze that he was furious.

Suddenly the distance between them seemed too great. She hurried toward him, and when she reached his side, he put his arm around her.

He asked, *Why are your shoes in the closet?*

She shivered. *We had an extra place setting, and I was looking for somewhere to stow it when I stepped inside and-and found him. I didn't want to track b-blood everywhere, or contaminate the scene any more than I already had, so I stepped out of them.*

He rubbed her back. "Okay. Now, I want you to go into the security room in the basement and stay there. Will you do that for me, please?"

She shook her head. "No."

"That's a good idea," Tiago said to Niniane. "You

could go too."

Dragos glared at her. "Pia. The vice president's husband was murdered *in our house.*"

She gave him an exasperated look. "Like I don't know that already! I am not going downstairs, so put a guard on me if you have to, but I'm staying up here to help."

Jered snapped, "Enough of this squabbling over who is going to run away. You need to catch the murderer immediately, before all our diplomatic chances are ruined."

Dragos rounded on the Djinn. "*I* need to catch the murderer? This has nothing to do with the Wyr."

The Djinn gave him an incredulous look. "You must be joking. The human male's throat was slashed just as a Wyr might do. And as you said, it happened in your house. This is your responsibility. You're involved whether you like it or not. And others will blame you—again, whether you like it or not. Hell, I don't even know who did it, and I blame you."

A hot burst of anger fired through Pia's veins. She snapped, "That's completely unfair! None of our people would do such a thing!"

The Djinn glanced at her. "Fairness has nothing to do with it. Appearances are everything." He turned back to Dragos. "You need to either find the murderer quickly, or you need to hide it. If you want someone to get rid of the body, I can do it."

"Bullshit," muttered Niniane. "He's *the vice president's husband*, Jered. You can't just whisk away the body!"

"This is a stupid conversation," Tiago said.

Jered rounded on him. "I see that you haven't come up with anything useful."

"*That's enough,*" Dragos hissed. As they all fell silent, he said to the others, "Leave. Go back to the others and mingle." As they hesitated, he said between his teeth, "You're wasting valuable time."

Niniane touched Pia's hand and said in her head, *I don't care how much Dragos snarls or tries to order everybody around. If you need me, call and I'll come.*

Thank you. Pia grasped her fingers briefly.

Even still, Niniane lingered until Tiago pulled her away. He told her, "Let's go. And you do not leave my side for anything, faerie. I mean you do not step two feet away from me."

"Oh, pffft," Niniane exclaimed, as she walked away with him.

"I think you're making a mistake not getting rid of the body," Jered said. With that parting shot, he strode after the other couple.

"For being such a bright people, sometimes the Djinn are remarkably clueless," Dragos muttered. He turned his attention to her. "Bayne's on his way. How long do we have until dinner is supposed to be served?"

Calculating rapidly, she said, "Soon. Maybe in five or six minutes. Gennita checked in with me just a little while ago, and I told her fifteen minutes. That was when I went to take the extra place setting off the table, and-and-and—"

Words seemed to stick in her throat as her brain

seized up again.

Giving her a sharp, questioning glance, Dragos put one bracing hand on her back again, right over the tense knot between her shoulder blades. Grateful for his silent touch, she managed to stop stuttering.

Bayne rounded the corner and strode toward them, his big body a fluid, fast machine. He didn't waste time asking questions when he reached them. Instead, he swept the scene quickly with those hard, hazel eyes, taking everything in, and then he turned to Dragos.

Pia was used to seeing Bayne smiling in a laid-back stance, usually with hands tucked into his jeans pockets. It always jarred her when the sentinels flipped some internal switch in their heads and went into warrior mode.

Dragos said to him, "Guard Pia. Go where she goes, no matter what."

"You got it," said Bayne.

Before Pia could mention that Eva was a perfectly adequate guard, thank you very much, Dragos added, "And Bayne? If necessary, you fly her out of D.C., and you don't stop flying until you both get back to the Tower."

So that was why Dragos wanted Bayne guarding her, not Eva. Eva was a highly trained, effective warrior, but her Wyr form was canine. Not only could Bayne fly, but he also had the strength to carry Pia in flight.

"Understood." Bayne turned that hard gaze to Pia, and his expression softened somewhat as he looked down the length of her body at her bare, smudged feet.

Furiously, Pia wanted to snap at both men for thinking they could decide her fate without her input, but she managed to catch herself up before she said anything she might regret later.

She wasn't thinking as rationally as she could be, and she knew Dragos wasn't either. He had seen a dead body and clicked into hyperprotective mode, and nothing was going to ratchet him down again until he felt like he had gained some measure of control over the situation.

There was that concept again – control over the situation. She glanced at dead Mr. Colton again and nearly burst into hysterical laughter. Like her going into hysterics was going to help anybody. She managed to swallow that impulse down too.

Dragos turned an incandescent gold gaze onto her. He said, "Stall dinner for as long as you can. Go."

She nodded. "Got it."

With Bayne on her heels, she ran barefoot to the kitchen, which was awhirl with activity. The kitchen staff was busy preparing the second course to follow the salmon soufflé, delicate grilled endive salads with light shavings of aged parmesan cheese and paper-thin Parma ham arranged in a fan on top.

She didn't try to talk over everybody else. Instead, she said telepathically, *Gennita, we need to stall dinner for at least another half hour. Longer, if possible.*

The chef spun to face her, eyes widening in dismay. *We can't stall dinner! The soufflés are almost done cooking!*

Normally she would be much more gentle with Gennita's wounded feelings, but now she didn't have the emotional or physical time. She told the other woman grimly, *We have much bigger problems right now than the soufflés. Get another round of hors d'oeuvres outside as fast as you can.*

But they're all gone! Gennita quivered visibly.

Pia threw up her hands. *Send out the salads then! Send out anything, along with more alcohol. Lots and lots of alcohol.*

Gennita rounded on her staff and started snapping out orders.

As Pia turned to Bayne, Eva slipped into the kitchen, caught sight of her and walked over. "When are you going to announce it's time to go into dinner?"

"I'm not," she said grimly. "Run upstairs and get me a pair of shoes."

Eva stared at her bare feet. "What happened to the ones you were wearing?"

"Later," she told Eva.

"But you only have one pair with you that matches that outfit. Which ones do you want?"

"I don't care!" she cried. "Shoes, get me shoes. Dark ones, that nobody will notice."

At that, Eva seemed to catch up with the fact that something had gone badly awry, because her expression changed until she looked much as Bayne did, bladelike and focused. She took off running.

"I need alcohol too," Pia told Bayne. She meant it desperately.

He took her at her word, strode over to the counter where the liquor bottles sat, swiped up a bottle of cognac and handed it to her.

She took a long pull, coughed and handed it back to

him. He drank from the bottle as well.

Gennita rushed up to her, wide eyes teary. "What should I do with the soufflés?"

Pia's gaze went unfocused. She stared into space a moment. Then she said, "Burn them."

The chef's expression quivered. "They're made with Balik Fillet Tsar Nikolaj smoked salmon. It costs $360 a pound. We can't just burn them."

"Yes, we can." Pushing past the other woman, she rushed over to the ovens and turned them to their highest settings.

Gennita followed behind her. "What are you doing?!"

Pia said between her teeth, "There are too many guests with sensitive noses. We need the smell of something burning to fill the air. And I need to be able to tell the truth when I go out there and say we've had a slight accident in the kitchen, and dinner's going to be a little later than we thought."

"That would never happen in real life," Gennita muttered. "Not in my kitchen."

"Nobody outside the Wyr knows that," Pia said. "At least I don't think."

Bayne dropped the cognac, and the bottle shattered on the floor. Everybody stopped what they were doing to stare at him.

He said, "Oops. Accident."

Eva loped back into the kitchen, carrying high heeled black pumps. Pia snatched at them and slipped them on her feet. She told Eva, "Find Dragos. Do whatever he needs."

"But . . ." The other woman paused. Normally Eva guarded Pia, no matter what. Clearly confused, she looked from Pia to Bayne.

"We're switching roles tonight," Bayne told her. "Go."

Eva shot out of the kitchen again.

Pia strode to the liquor counter, grabbed another bottle at random and took a healthy swig from it. The two hits of alcohol seemed to make the buzzing in her ears fade away, until she felt dizzy, with her head stuffed with cotton wool.

The first faint hint of an acrid smell filled the kitchen.

"Okay," she whispered. "Okay."

She waited another minute until the acrid smell grew stronger, and then, followed by Bayne, she strode outside with a big apologetic smile to face her powerful, intelligent, and not-altogether-friendly guests.

DRAGOS DIDN'T KNOW how Pia would stall things, and he didn't care. He just knew she would handle it.

Dismissing the issue from his mind, he concentrated on the problem at hand.

Problem equaling corpse, of course.

Bracing one hand on the doorway, he leaned into the closet without stepping inside, and inspected Colton. It was easier to do, now that he was by himself and not distracted by the others.

The dragon surfaced in his mind again, not at all perturbed by the unexpected dead body. He noted details.

He took note of faint whiffs of old scents, along with the scent of aged wood, and set them aside. The only new scents in the closet were Pia and, of course, Colton's copious blood, along with a faint, underlying hint of chemical stink.

Colton was wearing KO Odorless Odor Eliminator again, as was his wife. Dragos had taken note of it as soon as the Coltons had stepped into his house. He had also noted every other smiling guest who wore it.

All of them were his enemies. They knew it.

He knew it.

And one of them had murdered a man in his house.

Still leaning into the closet, he reached for the pen in his breast pocket. With the tip, he probed at the wounds on Colton's neck. There were five wounds, four on one side, and one on the other. As Jered so obnoxiously pointed out, on the surface at least, it did look like a Wyr kill.

Dragos was very familiar with the general pattern. The style of the wounds was reminiscent of a Wyr ripping out someone's throat with his talons. He had done it himself a number of times over the centuries, but if there was one thing he would stake his life on in that moment, it was that no Wyr present would *ever* betray him in his own house. Everyone on this trip was handpicked, either by Bayne or by himself. Only the highest-qualified Wyr, and the most loyal, had been chosen.

So, not only did someone who was wearing KO Odorless Odor Eliminator kill Colton, but they had somehow made it look like a Wyr had committed the murder. They had planned this very carefully. Bayne had installed the tiny security cameras in every room, but not in the hallways, and certainly not in any of the closets. The killer had murdered Colton in one of the blind spots.

Eyes narrowed, he probed deeper at one of the wounds. The flesh at the two edges of the cut fell apart cleanly. The wounds were almost surgical in their neatness. The blades had been very sharp.

Even still, the blood would have spurted until Colton's heart stopped. How had the murderer kept from getting blood on him—or her?

He looked more closely at the area around the body, at the closet floor and underneath the desk. There, he discovered a cheap pocket rain poncho stuffed behind the chair. He didn't bother to pull it out. If he did, he knew he would find it splattered with blood.

A footstep sounded nearby in the hall.

Sir, Eva said in his head. *I'm supposed to help you with whatever you need.*

Eva was smart to telepathize before trying to approach behind his back. He pulled back from the corpse and straightened to turn to her.

Two things, he said. *First, get security to search the house from top to bottom, and move fast. We're looking for a weapon, some kind of glove with razor blades attached to the tips of the fingers and thumbs. When it's found, let me know. I want photos taken. Nobody should move it or touch it with their bare hands.*

Standing on the balls of her feet, Eva looked sober and sharp, and ready to run as soon as he finished giving orders.

Second thing, he told her. *Get a list of people who disappeared from the security cameras nearest this location, from the time the guests arrived to*—he checked his watch—*about five minutes ago, when Pia walked down this hall. Tell them to move very fast. I want a list of possible suspects in the next fifteen minutes.*

Yes, sir. She bolted.

In the distance, his sharp hearing picked up Pia's voice outside, followed by what sounded like good-natured laughter. Almost at the same time, he noticed an acrid scent, like burning food, and he smiled to himself. She had dealt with the problem splendidly.

If he wasn't missed beforehand, Colton would definitely be missed when dinner was announced. Dragos needed to come up with a plan of action, because every moment right now was critical.

Coming to a decision, he closed the door, straightened his cuffs and strode down the hall. *Pia, please quietly ask the president to meet me in the library.*

Okay. Her mental voice sounded tense. *Our time just got shorter. Vice President Colton has started looking for her husband.*

It was bound to happen sooner or later, he told her. *By the way, what kind of fresh meat do we have in the kitchen?*

Don't tell me you're hungry.

She had been acting so shocky earlier, he was glad to

hear a hint of dark humor in her voice. *No*, he said. *But I would like to know if there is a very large cut of something, a roast perhaps, or a leg of lamb. Even a turkey would do. Whatever it is can't be frozen. If we do have anything, I need it in the library too.*

I'll check then go talk to the president.

Thank you. He paused for the briefest of moments. *Everything is going to be okay, you know. Even if we can't make this okay, we're going to be fine.*

Her voice warmed. *I know we will. I love you.*

I love you too, he told her.

He realized he didn't tell her that enough. She never complained or appeared to take hurt from it, but still, he made a note to tell her more often. He tried to show her how he felt, but she deserved the words too.

Stepping into the library, he poured himself a scotch, took a seat, crossed his legs and waited.

Shortly, one of the kitchen staff walked in briskly, carrying a tray that held a large, irregularly shaped item wrapped in butcher's paper. Following Dragos's orders, he set the tray on a round Chippendale table and left.

Within a few minutes, he heard Pia and Johnson chatting as they came near. They walked into the library, with Bayne and the president's guard following behind.

"You two," Dragos said to Bayne and the president's man. "Wait outside."

The Secret Security guard looked to the president, who gave him a nod. Only then did he move with Bayne to step outside the room.

Dragos added in Bayne's head telepathically, *Cordon off the area of hall where the body is. And nobody comes in this room without my say-so. Do you hear? I mean come hell or high water, nobody comes in here, and I expect things will get very unpleasant out there soon.*

I hear you, said Bayne, as he backed out of the room, closing the double doors to the hall. *Nobody's coming in, not even this nice, dedicated soldier standing with me right now, although I hope to gods I don't have to shoot him. I'll have George stand guard with us.*

George was part of Bayne's security detail, a massive, easygoing man who was also a rare Wyr elephant. As strong and stubborn as a troll, if George stood guard at the doors with Bayne, nobody would get in unless Dragos said they could.

Very good, Dragos said. Leisurely he stood. "Thank you for coming, Ben. Can I pour you a drink?"

The president laughed. "You've been very generous with the alcohol this evening, Dragos. I think I'd better pass on any more until we have some dinner."

"About that dinner," said Dragos.

As he spoke, he moved to the liquor tray, refreshed his drink and poured a second scotch for the president. With a quick glance at Pia, he raised his eyebrows at her in inquiry. She looked tense again, and very pale. Dark patches of feverish red touched her cheeks. Twisting her fingers together, she shook her head.

Johnson laughed again, only this time he sounded uneasier. He looked back and forth at Dragos and Pia. "Don't tell me there's been another kitchen accident."

"No, there hasn't." Dragos turned to face the president, holding both drinks. "I'm going to ask you for one thing—only one, but it's going to be hard for you for a little while."

"What's that?" President Johnson's intelligent expression had turned closed and wary.

Walking over to him, Dragos held out a scotch. "We need to have a frank, tough conversation, you and I. And whatever you may think, or however you may react while we're having it, I need for you to hear me out."

Chapter Nine

JOHNSON SEARCHED HIS gaze then turned to study Pia's anxious figure. His gaze fell to her twisted hands. "Okay," he said simply, reaching out to accept the scotch. "I believe we can have a civilized discourse. Now, what's this about?"

Here goes, Dragos thought. He met Pia's gaze as he said, "In the last hour and a half, one of your humans murdered the vice president's husband, and they tried to make it look like a Wyr did it."

Johnson's eyes narrowed, and his frame stiffened. "Murdered—Victor is *dead*?"

"Very dead," Dragos told him bluntly. He swallowed scotch. "His body is in a hall closet. The killer used some kind of glove with either razor blades or knives attached to the end of the fingers and thumb. My staff is looking for the murder weapon now. The motion used was an inward, slashing one, as if the killer went to grab Colton's throat one-handed, only instead of strangling him, he closed his fingers and yanked. The carotid arteries on both sides of Colton's throat were cut. He bled out within ninety seconds, tops."

Outside the library, someone called out. Dragos

could hear the vice president's voice in the distance, asking, *Have you seen Victor?*

Dragos tuned her out.

Johnson remained standing where he was, his tall, distinguished figure vibrating with reaction, expression blazing with shock and outrage. "Victor is dead, and you're claiming that a human did it?!"

"It's a fact, Ben," Dragos said. "I can prove it."

Turning, Dragos walked to the desk, set aside his scotch and began to unwrap the large piece of meat on the tray. When he had opened the package, he discovered it was a leg of lamb, nicely covered with a thin layer of white fat. Excellent. The fat would show every mark.

Pia moved to sit with a plop at one end of the sofa. Both she and Johnson watched Dragos, their expressions filled with fascination and repugnance.

"The killer was cunning," Dragos told them. "He put a great deal of planning into the murder. He dodged security cameras and made a murder weapon that would simulate a Wyr's capabilities. But he was stupid too. The murder weapon didn't simulate a Wyr's talons. Wyr handgrips are stronger than humans. Maybe he was concerned his human grip wouldn't be able to strike a killing blow. If I were him, I would have wanted to make sure I could cut the carotid arteries, so I would have been focused on making sure my blades were very sharp. That's what he did. Watch closely now—these are what my talons look like."

As Johnson and Pia stared, he held out one hand and made the slight shift that brought out his talons. Splaying his fingers, he held them up for the others to see.

Johnson said, "I've never seen that in person."

"Most people haven't," Dragos told him.

The president looked at Pia. "Do you have talons like that too?"

She shook her head with a smile that looked strained. "Only predator Wyr have talons like that. I'm an herbivore. I don't have the nature or the personality for it."

"You're perfectly safe, Ben," Dragos told the president. "You can step closer, if you like. Do you see how the talons are shaped?"

Fascination overtook Johnson's shock and outrage, and he took a few steps toward Dragos. "They're curved and angled to a point, from the fingertips to the tip."

"Exactly. They're extremely sharp, but they're also natural. They're made of a hard protein called keratin—which means they aren't exactly uniform either, not like a manufactured blade is. Watch what happens when I make a wound like the ones that killed Colton."

Striking quickly, Dragos grabbed hold of the leg of lamb. He had to pin the meat to the tray with one hand while he tightened his grip and pulled with the other. Flesh tore underneath his talons. Both Johnson and Pia flinched back, but when he was finished, they moved closer to stare at what lay on the tray.

Stepping away from the lamb to give them a little space, Dragos let his talons retract as he pulled out a handkerchief and wiped off his hands. It was getting noisy outside. Questions were being asked, along with demands.

Concentrating on his small task, he said, "This meat was refrigerated, so it's a little stiff, but it will still show you want I want you to see. If you look closely at the marks I just made, you'll see there is a bit of tear to them. The edges are jagged. It's hard to kill someone like this. It's messy. Likely as not, you'll tear out chunks of flesh when you do it." He looked up and met Johnson's sharp gaze. "Colton's wounds are not like this, Ben. They're surgical. The edges of the cuts are sharp. They were made with blades, not talons."

"Why are you telling me this, now?" Johnson asked. His shock and fear had receded, and he studied Dragos with his arms crossed.

"Because this is the single piece of evidence I have that will be the most compelling for you," Dragos told him. "The killer might have been cunning, but aside from being stupid, he was also bigoted and insulting. He believed the first thing anybody would think when they saw Colton would be that a Wyr had killed him. In my house, Ben. With my handpicked staff, my highly trained and reliable security. *With my wife present.* He believed that everybody would think the *Wyr* were that stupid. And he ignored the fact that none of us have any motive to commit this crime."

Only then did Dragos let his rage show. Pia swallowed hard, and Johnson's gaze flickered, but he didn't flinch or back down like he had a few moments ago.

A knock sounded at the door, and a man called out, "Mr. President, are you all right? The first lady is asking after you."

Johnson raised his voice. He sounded strong and steady. "Yes, Brock. We're all safe in here. I'll let you know when I'm done."

"Very good, sir."

Johnson said to Dragos, "So the wounds are the most compelling piece of evidence, you said. What other evidence do you have?"

"Other than Colton's blood and Pia's scent—she was the one who found him, by the way—there were no other scents. The killer was wearing KO Odorless Odor Eliminator. Only deer hunters wear the scent blocker, or Wyr criminals—and of course now anybody who is involved in the Right to Privacy movement is wearing it too." Dragos gave him a cynical smile. "But only the Wyr would know that or be able to make that claim, and nobody would be listening if we were the suspects. And the only people wearing KO Odorless Odor Eliminator here tonight are human. Your killer is one of the humans."

Johnson drew in a sharp breath. "Do you have any idea who the killer might be?"

Dragos shook his head. "No, and I don't care. At first I trapped myself into thinking I had to find the killer before Colton's murder was discovered, but then I realized—this isn't my problem. I'm insulted that the killer did this in my home, and I'm offended, but this is a human issue. And the fact that it happened during the one week when humans and the Elder Races were making an active effort to maintain good relations is disturbing. Aside from whatever the killer had against

Colton, someone doesn't want us to get along, Ben."

"My God, what a bloody mess," Johnson muttered. He rubbed his face and looked at Dragos over the tops of his fingers. "Okay, I believe you."

Dragos relaxed slightly. "Thank you," he said. "I appreciate that. My staff has been looking for the murder weapon, but they have instructions to take photos only and not to disturb anything if they find it. And security has been reviewing recordings of who disappeared from view from the cameras placed in the rooms during the time that the murder took place."

"I need that list," Johnson said. "Along with footage of the recordings to back it up." His somber expression turned sour. "And I would appreciate a list of all the people who came here wearing that scent blocker. Up until now, I've ignored the Right to Privacy movement, as I thought it would blow over once we got things on a better footing, but not anymore."

Johnson might have the luxury of ignoring it up until now, but Dragos, for one, wouldn't be ignoring anything to do with the Right to Privacy movement. In fact, he planned on investigating it thoroughly and having extensive dossiers created on every prominent person involved.

"Of course," Dragos told him. "You'll get the full list of everyone I noted, so you can compare it with the shortlist compiled from the security footage. Your killer will be one of the humans on the shortlist. And naturally, we'll open our home up to your people for a thorough investigation."

"Thank you." Johnson stepped forward and extended his hand. Dragos shook it. "And thank you for your calm and incisive thinking, and for your help as the authorities resolve this matter."

"You're welcome," Dragos told him. When Johnson made as if to withdraw, he maintained his grip until the other man met his gaze. "It's important to me that we remain allies, Ben, just as it is important to every other demesne leader here, which is why we've all come. But make no mistake—we're not here because we're apologetic. We're here because we're concerned about Elder Races violence, just as we're also concerned about human abuses and violence—the hundreds of people killed in school and theater shootings, and the thousands killed in terrorist attacks. Violence against police, along with police bigotry and brutality, and the tragedy of what happened at Devil's Gate. We're willing to work together with you as partners to lessen these incidents, but none of us are willing to become scapegoats."

The president's expression tightened, but he gave Dragos a short nod. "Understood."

As Dragos released the other man's hand, for the first time in a long time, Pia spoke up telepathically. She said softly in his head, *You're sexy when you're incisive and imperious.*

The dragon in his head hadn't receded and preened at the compliment from his mate. He gave her a sidelong smile as he told her, *I didn't know how the conversation was going to go or how difficult it might get. All I knew was that we needed to walk out of this room allies, but Johnson also needed to know—the Elder Races aren't going to be his bitch, just because some humans decided to throw a hissy.*

That's my dragon politician I know and love so well, she crooned.

He laughed softly. They watched as Johnson squared his shoulders, strode for the double doors and threw them open.

A noisy crowd of guests had gathered outside in the hall. Tumultuous noise blasted into the room, as everyone tried to talk or shout at once. The president stepped forward and raised his voice to address them.

Pia rolled her eyes and said, *I can't even deal with all the drama llama.*

As Dragos cocked an amused eyebrow at her, she collapsed in a dead faint.

✧ ✧ ✧

PIA DREAMED THE dragon coiled around her in a white heat and raged at anybody else who tried to come close. All the protestors with their slogans and placards had to remain outside on the sidewalks.

You're not helping any, she tried to tell him. *We need to get the dinner on the table, or the soufflés will be ruined. We can serve Mr. Colton in the closet. There's already a place setting on the desk.*

But she was wrapped in thick cotton wool that made it impossible for her to move or say the words out loud.

Then the dragon picked her up and raced around with her, as they searched for her spinach soufflé so that she could eat it before it fell flat. *I'm not hungry*, she wanted to tell him, while in the kitchen, Gennita sniffled over the endive salad.

The Djinn Soren appeared in a swirl of Power, but he was a member of the Elder tribunal. He wasn't one of the demesne leaders, and they didn't have a place at the table for him.

"Bring Wyr doctors," the white-faced dragon told him. "And Soren, I swear to all the gods, if you try to bargain with me right now, I'll—"

"I will return as quickly as I can," said the Djinn, his starlike gaze fixed on Pia. His physical form disappeared.

And then there was blood, so much blood. She cried and wrung her hands, because her shoes were ruined, and she didn't have time to wash her feet.

That brought the dragon's attention back to her. Somehow they had arrived in an unfamiliar bedroom. She couldn't figure out whose house she was in. As she lay stretched out on the bed, he bent over her prone figure and placed a hot hand on her forehead.

"Hush, darling," he murmured. "Don't cry so. Everything will be all right."

Suddenly the dragon vanished, and it was Dragos stroking her forehead, Dragos, who looked stark and on the edge of panic.

She didn't think she had ever seen Dragos in a panic before. That frightened her more than anything she could have imagined. *Don't go*, she said, trying to reach through the cotton wool to take his hand. *Don't leave me.*

Strong fingers closed over hers. They were as hot as

the hand stroking her hair. "What nonsense are you talking now?" he whispered gently. "I could never leave you. Pia, you're hallucinating."

Rousing, she finally managed to get verbal words out of her mouth. "I am not," she told him in a strong voice. "There is too a dead man in our closet."

Well, in somebody's closet. She was pretty sure they weren't at home. If only she could remember where they were, and why.

"Ssh," he told her. "None of that matters right now."

She huffed. Easy for him to say. He's not the one who raced around like a crazy person all day trying to pull off the most important dinner party of his life.

Dr. Medina appeared in her line of sight, just behind Dragos's shoulder. Okay, maybe she really was hallucinating, because she hadn't even called the doctor back yet.

"Get out of my way, Dragos," the doctor said.

He moved away quickly, and the doctor leaned over to smile at Pia. "Just relax, dear," she said, showing Pia the glove she wore. The one with five blades on the end of the fingers and thumb. "You won't feel a thing."

As she opened her mouth, true darkness rose up to swallow her scream.

Chapter Ten

WHEN SHE NEXT opened her eyes, she found herself in their bedroom in D.C., tucked underneath the covers. She ached everywhere, like she had the flu or someone had beaten her in every major muscle group.

The room was still a mess, clothes strewn everywhere. The curtains were pulled, with no hint of sunlight along the edges, but the bedside lamp on Dragos's side of the bed was on, throwing a circle of warm illumination into the room.

Dragos lay stretched out on his back beside her on top of the covers, fully clothed in black jeans and a black silk sweater. He had the fingers of one hand draped over his eyes, while he held her hand with the other.

She could hear several voices in the distance, along with movement, both inside the house and out. Someone slammed a car door outside.

She squeezed Dragos's fingers, and he erupted upright to bend over her, eyes blazing. He called out, "Medina, she's awake."

Almost immediately, the bedroom door opened, and Dr. Medina stepped inside. "I'm here."

Briefly, Pia considered sitting up, but it seemed like too much effort. "I thought you were a dream," she told the doctor in a rusty voice.

Dr. Medina smiled at her. "You were pretty confused when I arrived."

"You fainted," Dragos told her. Lines of tension scored his face. "Scared centuries off my life when I saw you collapse like a rag doll."

Contritely, she squeezed his fingers as she thought back. "We were with the president in the library. How long ago was that?"

"Last evening. It's almost dawn now. Investigators have been here all night." Dragos touched her face, stroking the curve of her cheek. "How do you feel?"

She admitted, "Achy."

"Do you need anything, perhaps a drink of water?"

"Maybe in a bit," she sighed. His caress was so soothing, it made her want to close her eyes again.

Dragos turned a hard expression to the doctor. "You said you would talk to us both when Pia woke up. Well, she's awake now, so start talking."

The doctor gave him a look of rebuke. "I also told you she was going to be okay." She turned to Pia. "And you *are* going to be okay. Do you feel up to having a conversation right now, or do you need more rest?"

Beside her, Dragos felt so tight, like he was going to explode. Remembering the raging dragon from her dream—hallucination—she nodded. She did need more rest, but she didn't think he could hold off any longer.

"Okay," said Dr. Medina, straightening. "I have

some great news and some not very great news for you, and it's all tied together. Remember, the most important thing is—you're going to be okay, and so is your baby."

"*What?*" Pia said, not believing what she had just heard. Was she hallucinating again? She glanced sideways at Dragos, who looked as thunderstruck as her. "I'm not pregnant. I can't be pregnant."

Swiftly, Dragos placed one large hand over her flat stomach. She felt his Power probing deep within her. Placing her hand over his, she sank her awareness deep into her body too.

"I don't sense anything," Dragos said.

Pia muttered, "I don't either."

Dr. Medina folded her arms and regarded them both with a certain wry, sour expression. "You're not really questioning my diagnosis, are you? The last I heard, neither one of you had a medical license."

"But I'm not feeling anything." She felt close to tears. "Does that mean something's wrong?"

"*Wait.*" Dragos leaned closer, his expression arrested. "Fuck me. I've got it."

"I don't feel it! I can't sense anything." Frantically she searched harder, but she couldn't feel a thing, not until Dragos's Power surrounded her awareness and drew her attention to . . .

A slight something, nestled deep, hardly more than a shadow. Catching her breath, she strained everything she could toward that subtle shadow but couldn't pick up any more details.

She would have missed it entirely if it hadn't been for

Dragos pointing it out.

And Dragos had missed it entirely until the doctor told them.

"Can you feel it now?" Dragos asked.

"Yes, but what does it mean?" she whispered anxiously. "Liam didn't feel anything like this."

An incredulous smile lit Dragos's hard features, and his gold gaze flashed up to hers. "I think the little shit's cloaking itself. And its cloaking ability is so damn good, it fooled even me."

Pia's gaze flew to the doctor's, who nodded in confirmation. Wonder coursed through her tired body, along with a tumultuous cascade of joy.

She said to Dragos, "You *do* have mighty sperm. Once we made the decision, we must have gotten pregnant on our very first *pow*."

He kissed her swiftly but sobered as he turned back to face Dr. Medina. "You said there was not so great news."

"Yes, well." The doctor looked down at her feet and pursed her lips. "Remember this, and keep it firmly fixed in your mind—you're going to be okay, and the baby is going to be okay."

Pia's anxiety came back, squashing the incredulous joy. Not wanting to hear what came next while she was lying flat on the bed, she pushed herself upright. "What is it? Why have I felt so sick and had so many symptoms?"

"Sometimes, when a predator and an herbivore are mated, complications can arise," Dr. Medina told them.

"Sometimes those complications turn serious. You remember how nauseated you were during your pregnancy with Liam?"

She snorted. "I'll never forget it. I was sick every time I took my necklace off."

"You can roughly compare this situation to when a human mother has a different Rh factor in her blood than her baby." The doctor paused. "Have you heard of that before?"

Dragos shook his head, but Pia nodded. "I've heard of it."

Dr. Medina looked at her. "Often there's no problem with the first child a mother has, but during the pregnancy she develops antibodies to carrying the fetus, so there can be complications with the second child. Those can get severe."

"What are you saying?" Pia asked, gripping Dragos's hand tightly. "Are you saying I've developed antibodies to carrying Dragos's fetuses?"

"That's a simple way to put it, but yes, you have," the doctor replied. "And your symptoms appeared much more quickly and are more extreme."

"But you said they would be all right," Dragos said sharply.

"And they will." Dr. Medina turned to her and said forcefully, "You *will*. We will make sure of it. There is no reason at all to panic over this. You will do everything you did for Liam's pregnancy. You will eat right, exercise when you feel good and whenever possible avoid stress. Last night I treated you with spells to dampen your symptoms. I can also develop a drug protocol specifically targeted to suppress your antibodies, so that your body doesn't reject the baby. We will monitor this pregnancy very closely. That means examinations every two weeks, so that we can make adjustments if necessary."

Pia tried to calm the shaking in her limbs. "Okay," she said unsteadily. She tried to smile at Dragos. "We can do that. It's going to be okay."

"Yes," he said simply. "Nothing else is acceptable."

But Pia could tell—they both felt too much on edge, too close to disaster to really settle, which was why, when Dr. Medina took a deep breath, they turned to her so quickly.

"Now for the not so great news," Dr. Medina said.

Pia felt her stomach bottom out. She whispered, "I thought *that* was the not so great news."

The doctor gave her a kind smile. "That was part of it. The other part is—and there's no easy way to say this—Pia, this has got to be your last pregnancy. I'm very sorry to tell you this, but if you try to get pregnant a third time, as extreme as your reaction has become, the likelihood is, you'll miscarry it almost right away. You would almost certainly miscarry with this pregnancy too over the next month or two, if you hadn't received medical attention—which you *have*, and you and this baby are *just fine*. But if you were to try for a third pregnancy, you'll only put yourself at risk and both you and Dragos through a great deal of heartache. I can help you bring this baby to term, but I can't help you with another one."

Pia held herself still, absorbing the news. After a moment, she said, "Is that all of it?"

"Yes, pretty much."

She bit her lip as she looked from Dr. Medina to Dragos. "I was so sure I wasn't pregnant, I took a couple of doses of antihistamines yesterday. Is that a problem?"

The doctor shook her head. "Not at all. Some human drugs work well for Wyr, and that happens to be one of them. And since you're *not* human, you can enjoy everything that you did when you were pregnant with Liam, including wine and alcohol, since there's no placental transfer of alcohol for expectant Wyr mothers."

She expelled a quick sigh of relief and the stiffness went out of her spine.

Dr. Medina continued, "I want you on bed rest for the next two days, so that your system can recover from the symptoms you've developed while I get your protocol developed. Then you can take your first dose. I've been making arrangements through the night for my other patients, and I've set up temporary privileges at Georgetown Hospital while you remain in D.C. That's where I'm going in a few hours to work on creating your protocol, so I'll be on hand if you need me. If you have any questions or concerns, you've got me on speed dial. Until then, calm down, don't stress, eat lots of lovely good food and enjoy your new pregnancy with that very intriguing mystery you've got baking in your oven." Dr. Medina's gaze slid to Dragos. "And let your husband pamper you."

"I can't thank you enough," Pia told her.

Dr. Medina touched her shoulder. "It's my pleasure, Pia. I'll leave you two alone now."

When the door shut behind her, Pia sat for a moment, absorbing everything the doctor had said.

Then she whirled around to throw her arms around Dragos, her face suffused with glee. "Oh my God, we're really pregnant! Part of me was so convinced it wasn't ever going to happen!"

His arms came around her, crushing her ribs, he held her so tightly. He rasped, "When you fainted like that, you scared the shit out of me."

"I know, I'm so sorry." She stroked the back of his head.

Pulling back, he kissed her hard, several times, then hugged her tightly again and rocked her.

Compulsively, she put her hand on her stomach and sought once more for that subtle shadow. When she found it, joy thrilled through her again. "You didn't by any chance get a glimpse of what sex it is, did you?"

"No. It's cloaking too tightly." Catching what she did, one corner of his mouth lifted as he said, "He's sneaky."

"Or she's discreet," she told him. "Oh my God, I really didn't think we could do it—and I certainly didn't think we could do it so soon."

Dragos's smile died. He asked, "How do you feel about the rest of what the doctor told us?"

She sobered too as she considered. After a few minutes, she said, "You know, I feel good. I'm still in shock that we actually *got* pregnant, and I'm just relieved to know that the baby and I are fine." She caught a glimpse of his face and added quickly, "And we're going to continue to be fine. As far as the rest of it goes . . . Dragos, we're lucky that we have one child, let alone that we're going to have two. I think—I'm not going to lie, I think it's going to make me sad sometimes. But if that happens, it will be far in the future, and all I will have to do is look at the two beautiful children we do have and I'll be able to remind myself how lucky we are. Besides, if we get ever desperate to have another baby around, we can always adopt." She sneaked a peek at his frowning expression. "How about you?"

"As long as you're okay, everything is okay even when it's not." Unsmiling, he met her gaze. "When you're not okay, the world is hell."

He had tightened one hand into a fist. She laid her hand over it, remembering the raging dragon in her hallucinations. She said gently, "And I'm okay. I'm more than okay, I'm over the moon."

"Despite feeling achy?" He passed one hand over her hair, tucking it behind her shoulder.

"This is worth feeling achy any day of the week." Somewhere, a door slammed again, reminding her of the outside world and its concerns. "What happened while I was out of it?"

He made a face and gesture that sliced through air. "Drama llamas."

"What?" She laughed.

The stress had begun to lift from his face, which she was glad to see. He cocked an eyebrow at her. "Don't you remember what you said just before you collapsed?"

She thought back then shook her head. "No, I'm afraid not."

"You rolled your eyes and said, 'I can't even deal with the drama llama.'" He chuckled then rubbed his eyes. "It wasn't funny at the time, though, dammit."

"I'm so sorry." She leaned against him, and he shifted to put his back against the headboard while keeping one arm around her. She curled against his side, one leg draped across his hips. "Do they have any idea who did it? Who killed Colton, I mean?"

After a moment, he told her, "After studying the footage from the cameras, security narrowed the suspects down to three people—Aaron Davis, Janice Wilmington and the speaker's security detail. And a few hours ago, they found the murder weapon. It was exactly what I thought, a gauntlet with curved blades welded to the ends of the fingers and thumbs. The murderer had it custom made."

She shuddered at the thought. "Where was it?"

"The killer had pried up a board and stuffed it under the floor in one of the bathrooms."

"I know we own this house, but I'm so glad this didn't happen in our actual home," she told him. "I would feel so violated if it had."

His hold tightened. "We would never have had any of those assholes in our home."

"True." She had to think a moment to place the names with titles and faces. Aaron Davis was the vice president's chief of staff, Janice Wilmington was the majority leader. She couldn't remember what the speaker of the House's security detail looked like. Curiously, she asked, "Who do you think did it?"

"I'm positive it was one of the two men, Davis or the security guy. Colton was a tall man. Wilmington isn't tall enough to have inflicted the wounds on him, at least not at the angle the cuts at his throat were made. As for why, I really don't give a damn. I just want them all out of my house and gone for good."

He pressed his mouth to her forehead, and they rested for several minutes.

"Bed rest for two days." She sighed. "I didn't bring any books with me. I thought I was going to be too busy to read this week."

"I'll go out and get you something to read tomorrow," he whispered. He began rubbing her back in long, soothing strokes. In no time, she grew sleepy and relaxed.

"Pregnant," she murmured. "I feel so gleeful about that, I could bust. We're pregnant, and we have no idea what it is."

"I could try to scan again, but I don't want to force it," he said quietly.

"No, I don't either. He or she will come out from behind that cloak when they're ready." She smiled sleepily. "Not knowing is kind of fun, kind of like a Masque or Christmas present."

"What an interesting future we're going to have," Dragos said. "I'd like to keep the news to ourselves for a little while, if you don't mind. Let's just enjoy it for a few weeks, then we can tell Liam and our close circle. Is that all right with you?"

"That sounds perfect."

This time she fell asleep peacefully, and she had no more bad dreams.

LATE THE NEXT morning, when she woke up, Dragos was still in bed with her, although he had showered and dressed, she saw, when she rolled over. He was busy reading some kind of typed report, which he set aside as she gave him a sleepy smile.

"What are you doing here?" she asked in a sleep-blurred voice as she stretched. All the muscle aches had eased, allowing her freedom of motion. "Why aren't you at—what was supposed to happen this morning? I can't remember it now."

He raised his eyebrows at her. "You collapsed last night, remember? I get to stay at home today to make sure you're recovering."

"Hmm." She hummed contentedly as she lifted her face for his kiss.

"Are you hungry?"

She nodded, and as he called down to the kitchen to order her some breakfast, she sat up in bed. Across the room, a high pile of wrapped presents sat on the table. "What are those for?"

"Those are for someone who is newly pregnant and can't leave her bed for two days." He lounged back against the headboard, looking sexy and wicked. "They'll be fun to look at until you can go get them, won't they?"

She rounded on him with a look of utter betrayal. "You wouldn't!"

He laughed. "No, I wouldn't."

"Well, okay then," she grumbled, subsiding. "Besides, I can't stay in bed for the entire two days without getting up. I've got to go to the bathroom and brush my teeth."

She did so, and she also washed the remnants of last night's makeup off her face, while he carried the presents to the bed. She felt shaky while she was on her feet, and when she was done with her toilette, she was glad to crawl back between the covers.

Then she opened presents while Dragos handed them to her, one by one. Sexy lingerie, a half a dozen books, several magazines, and *ooh* look, a beautiful pair of aquamarine earrings, vegan chocolates, a warm chenille robe, and a new tablet.

He had noticed that she had broken the screen of the tablet she had at home.

Warmed again by his attention and thoughtfulness, she turned to kiss him. "Thank you."

"You're welcome. I can buy you a TV too and have a dresser moved in to set it on, if you want."

She looked around the lovely, historical bedroom. "Thanks, but no, I like the bedroom this way. I can always watch things on the tablet if I feel like it."

"Well, let me know if you change your mind." Tilting her face further, he kissed her again. "I hope this all helps with the bed rest."

"It does," she promised.

The next day, he left her to join in the normal meetings and activities for the week. He texted her often, while she slept far more than she thought she would—she was still so tired—and nibbled on chocolates, and read.

The enforced bed rest also gave her a chance to really think about what the doctor had said, but even after a bout of soul-searching, the only real reaction she had was one of deep relief that she had actually fainted, which had gotten her the medical attention she needed before she could miscarry.

"Because you're the most important thing," she whispered to the tiny shadow nestled deep inside her. "The absolutely most important thing."

Also, if she were to be honest in the privacy of her own thoughts, she wasn't sorry at all that she got to miss two days of the week's activities. Only the thought of worrying Dragos would keep her from pretending to be sick so that she could get out of a third day as well.

For now, she was quite content to keep up with the latest happenings through Dragos's texts and by watching news shows on her new tablet, which was how she discovered that the police had made an arrest in the murder case.

It was early in the evening on the second day. Dr. Medina had given her the first shot of the drug protocol and cleared her for normal activities in the morning.

Eva lounged on the bed with her, reading and keeping her company while Dragos attended yet another dinner. Bored, Pia had run a Google search on Victor

Colton's death. To avoid disturbing Eva, she popped an earbud into one ear and clicked on the CNN link that promised BREAKING NEWS.

After watching a few minutes of the segment, she sat up straight and said, "Holy shit."

"What is it?" Eva looked up from her mystery.

Her eye glued to the small screen, she muttered, "They arrested Aaron Davis, the vice president's chief of staff. . . . There's allegations of an affair with the vice president, who's denying it. . . ." She pulled the earbud out of her ear and looked at Eva with round eyes. "This is very bad news for the White House administration, but it might be very good news for us."

Later, when Dragos walked into the bedroom, he was smiling.

Pia stopped her Fruit Ninja game and set her tablet aside. "You look like a cat that got away with something."

He pulled off his tie, shrugged out of his suit jacket and threw them into a chair. Toeing off his shoes, he rolled up his shirt sleeves and crawled up the bed to give her a kiss. And all of that was so damn sexy, she could have climaxed just by watching him.

Delighted to see him, she burrowed back against her pillows, kissing him back. He said against her mouth, "I missed you."

"I missed you too." When he pulled back, she smiled at him. "Did you hear the news about Aaron Davis's arrest?"

"Oh, hell yeah. Things couldn't be going better if I

had arranged them, myself."

As well as she thought she knew him, he had quite the capacity for surprising her. She squinted one eye at him. "You didn't, did you?"

"No, but I almost wish I had thought of it. The vice president is now being accused of starting the Right to Privacy movement as a setup for the murder. She's going to have to resign, or Ben will be forced to get rid of her. And nobody was wearing a scent blocker this evening."

She sighed. "That's a huge relief."

"It doesn't solve all our problems." He rubbed his face. "There's still plenty of protestors to the week's summit, and we're facing plenty of guarded government officials in our meetings. Senator Jackson is in clear opposition to mending fences, and public opinion is still on the downturn from the Nightkind massacre. But this latest development has slowed the momentum of the backlash against us, and I don't think we'll need to immigrate to our Other Greenland just yet, although I did talk to Niniane about hiring some consultants. She's going to send some people when she gets back to Adriyel." He slid back down the bed to put his head on her stomach. "How are you two doing?"

"We're great." She threaded her fingers through his black, silky hair. "And I'm excited that I get to go off bed rest in the morning."

"I'm excited too." He tilted his head so that he could look up at her. "Did the doctor clear you for normal activities?"

"I know what you really mean." She tapped his nose

with one finger. "And yes, I'm cleared to resume normal activities in the morning."

He grabbed her finger and kissed it. "I can't wait. And you got your shot. How do you feel?"

"I feel tired again, and my arm hurts a bit, but Dr. Medina said that's all normal. She said she can give me the shot every two weeks in the evening, so I can just go to bed afterward." She made a face and shrugged. "It's not a big deal."

"I'm glad to hear it." He didn't let go of her hand. Instead, he rubbed her fingers against his mouth.

Warmth spread through her at the gentle caress. She urged, "Tell me what else is new."

"You've already heard the great news this evening," he said against her fingers. "But there is also some not so great news, too."

"Oh, no." Her heart sank. "What's happened now?"

"Today we were talking about what measures the demesne leaders could take that would lessen the risk of violence instigated by the Elder Races, and some goddamn fool in Ben's administration got the bright idea that we could 'foster good will and peace among the demesnes' by having all seven leaders commit to sending a family member to visit another demesne for a week sometime in the next six months."

"That's ridiculous," she exclaimed. "It sounds exactly like some stupid, useless program the government would come up with. That's like the nobility who used to send their children to live with other nobles as hostages. What do they think, that we're living in the Middle Ages?"

He cocked a sardonic eyebrow. "That's precisely where they said they got the idea. Several of us objected most strenuously, but after a lengthy argument, it was put to a vote. The majority agreed to the measure." He frowned and growled, "I hate decisions by consensus."

"But you only have two family members, me and Liam. Well, you have three now, but the littlest one isn't going anywhere without me for a really long time, and I'm telling you right now, Dragos—Liam is not going to visit any other demesne on his own. I don't care how many bodyguards you put on him."

"Of course he isn't." Dragos's frown hadn't lessened.

"Which leaves me," she said flatly. "Of course."

"That was acknowledged in the meeting." He paused. "Almost everybody at our dinner party saw you faint two nights ago, and know you're on bed rest for some mysterious ailment, so Niniane pushed to extend the time limit on the Wyr visitation, and the others agreed. You now have a year, which does us no good whatsoever, because you'll have the baby then."

"Ugh, this is awful," she stared at him. "Do I at least get to pick where I go, and who I visit? I could go see Niniane in Chicago."

He rolled to his feet and strode over to a small liquor cart tucked into a corner. As he poured himself a scotch, he said, "No such luck. The fuckers drew straws."

The space over her left eye was beginning to throb. She pressed against it with three fingers. "Don't tell me I'm supposed to go visit the Elves again."

"Nope. You're supposed to visit the Light Fae demesne in Los Angeles. Tatiana told me to tell you, she's delighted."

"And I'm supposed to spend an entire week with her?" She threw up her hands. *"Oy vey."*

He tossed back his drink and poured another. "I didn't want to fucking talk about it anymore, so I shut up. But we're not going to comply. *Nobody* tells me where I should send my family."

She flung herself back on her pillows in exasperation and stared at the ceiling. If he did that, an idea that was supposed to *foster good will and peace among the demesnes, HA!* would end up causing more bickering and discord than ever.

"Stop," she said. "If we dig in our heels, it will only create the kind of resentment the whole damn thing is supposed to alleviate. It's not worth it. I'll go."

Angling his head, Dragos turned to look at her. "No, you bloody well won't."

She just looked at him. "Come on, it'll only be for a week. We'll suck it up and get it over with."

But she knew better than to say, what's the worst that could happen? Because they already saw how badly that could go, when she went to visit the Elves earlier that year.

He was wearing that stubborn expression of his that said he wasn't going to budge, no matter what. "You're not going anywhere without me. Period. And I wasn't invited."

She started to laugh. "When has that ever stopped you from doing anything?"

Did his scowl lessen just the tiniest bit? "Well, that's true."

"Let me get this straight—did anybody tell you that you *couldn't* go?"

The fierce scowl disappeared, and he began to smile. "It was implied, but actually, no."

"Well, there you are, then," she said. "We got all wound up over this for nothing."

Although it wasn't easy to sneak a dragon-sized critter across demesne borders, they would manage. Somehow, they always did.

Setting aside the scotch, he strolled back to bed. "Who knew that marrying a sneaky penny thief would come in so handy?"

"Hey," she said. "Discreet."

"That too." He stripped off his clothes, climbed into bed and turned off his light. Pia turned on her side so that he could spoon her from behind. He stroked her hair back and kissed her neck. "Time to get to sleep," he whispered in her ear. "We want to make sure you get all your rest out by morning."

Sleepy glee suffused her. Pretending to be clueless, she whispered back, "What's going to happen in the morning?"

"Oh, you know," he told her. "'You diddle here, I suck there. Or maybe you suck, and I diddle. Or both. Couple of pats, and ten or fifteen thrusts. Oh baby, you're so good, I can't take it, *pow*, et cetera, let's go raid the fridge.'"

Nodding in contentment, she closed her eyes. "That's what I hoped you would say."

Thank you!

Dear Readers,

Thank you for reading my short story *Dragos Goes to Washington*. Dragos, Pia and Liam Cuelebre are some of my favorite characters, and I'm delighted to share this new story with you. I hope you have as much fun visiting with them as I did!

Would you like to stay in touch and hear about new releases? You can:

- Sign up for my monthly email at: www.theaharrison.com
- Follow me on Twitter at @TheaHarrison
- Like my Facebook page at facebook.com/TheaHarrison

Reviews help other readers find the books they like to read. I appreciate each and every review, whether positive or negative.

Dragos Goes to Washington is the first story in a three-story arc featuring Dragos, Pia and their son Liam. The second story is *Pia Does Hollywood* (to be released on November 17th, 2015), and the third is *Liam Takes Manhattan* (December 22nd release). While each story is written so that it can be enjoyed individually, the reading experience will be stronger if you enjoy all three in order.

Happy reading!
Thea

Coming Soon on November 17th:

Pia Does Hollywood

(A Story of the Elder Races)

After making a diplomatic pact with humankind and the other leaders of the Elder Races, Pia Cuelebre, mate to Dragos Cuelebre, Lord of the Wyr, reluctantly heads to Hollywood to spend a week with the Light Fae Queen, Tatiana, before the busy Masque season hits New York in December.

Dragos has never let the lack of an invitation stop him from doing anything he wanted. Unwilling to let his mate make the trip without him, he travels to southern California in secret to be with her.

But when an ancient enemy launches a shattering assault against the Light Fae, Dragos and Pia must intercede. The destruction threatens to spread and strike a mortal blow against all of the magically gifted, both human and Elder Race alike.

Working with the Light Fae to neutralize the danger, Dragos and Pia find their deepest vulnerabilities challenged and their most closely held secrets threatened with exposure.

Pia Does Hollywood is the second part of a three-story series about Pia, Dragos, and their son, Liam. Each story stands alone, but fans might want to read all three: *Dragos Goes to Washington, Pia Does Hollywood*, and *Liam Takes Manhattan.*

Coming Soon on December 22, 2015:

Liam Takes Manhattan

(A Story of the Elder Races)

This is a short story (15,000 words or 50 pages) intended for readers of the Elder Races who enjoy Liam Cuelebre as a character.

Reeling from a deep loss, the magical prince of the Wyr, Dragos and Pia's son Liam Cuelebre, turns inward and withdrawn as he struggles to come to terms with who he is, along with the challenges that lie before him.

Hoping to ease his heartache and offer comfort, a concerned Dragos and Pia offer him a gift, something he has desired for a long time. Liam's response has a ripple effect across all of New York. Soon miracles of all kinds start arriving just in time for Christmas, along with a visit from a mysterious person who gives Liam hope and a vision of his future.

Liam Takes Manhattan is the third part of a three-story series about Pia, Dragos, and their son, Liam. Each story stands alone, but fans might want to read all three: *Dragos Goes to Washington, Pia Does Hollywood*, and *Liam Takes Manhattan.*

Look for these titles from Thea Harrison

THE ELDER RACES SERIES – FULL LENGTH NOVELS

Published by Berkley

Dragon Bound

Storm's Heart

Serpent's Kiss

Oracle's Moon

Lord's Fall

Kinked

Night's Honor

Midnight's Kiss

Shadow's End

ELDER RACES NOVELLAS

Published by Samhain Publishing

True Colors

Natural Evil

Devil's Gate

Hunter's Season

The Wicked

OTHER WORKS BY THEA HARRISON

Dragos Takes a Holiday

Pia Saves the Day

Peanut Goes to School

GAME OF SHADOWS SERIES

Published by Berkley

Rising Darkness

Falling Light

ROMANCES UNDER THE NAME AMANDA CARPENTER

E-published by Samhain Publishing

(original publication by Harlequin Mills & Boon)

A Deeper Dimension

The Wall

A Damaged Trust

The Great Escape

Flashback

Rage

Waking Up

Rose-Coloured Love

Reckless

The Gift of Happiness

Caprice

Passage of the Night

Cry Wolf

A Solitary Heart

The Winter King

Made in the USA
San Bernardino, CA
15 January 2016